THE BOHEMIAN PIRATE

ALSO BY SARAH LAWSON

MEMOIR

A Fado for my Mother
The Ripple Effect

POETRY

Below the Surface
All the Tea in China
The Wisteria's Children

TRANSLATION

Christine de Pisan, *The Treasure of the City of Ladies*
René de Laudonnière, *A Foothold in Florida*
Jacques Prévert, *Selected Poems*
Leandro Fernández de Moratín, "The Girls' Consent"
Sera Anstadt, *All My Friends Are Crazy*

THEATRE

"Gertrude, Queen of Denmark"

THE BOHEMIAN PIRATE

SARAH LAWSON

CONTENTS

THE BOHEMIAN PIRATE

You can find anything when you're lost, it's just not always the thing you were looking for. If you went looking for The Bohemian Pirate you would be lucky to find it, but if you happened to walk down a side street behind King Edward College and turn into an even smaller street and then into a pretty little paved courtyard, you couldn't miss it. When they finally put up the blue Dutch awning the place was more noticeable, assuming you had found the courtyard in the first place. My brother Swithin used to go there a lot during term time, but especially during that summer when he was trying to write his book and the College was really out of commission because of the renovation work. At The Bohemian Pirate business was slack out of term time and Swithin could sit at a table and get on with his book undisturbed. It was a miracle that he ever finished writing the book, because in fact there were quite a few disturbances. He used to tell me about some of the people he met, just sitting at his table. Swithin used to say that the sight of someone sitting in a public place reading a book or writing something attracted talkative people.

By the time I went to King Edward, The Bohemian Pirate had changed hands and they had put up chintz café curtains but the blue awning was still there. Sometimes now you see it mentioned in those where-to-get-a-good-cup-of-coffee-in-London guides. In Swithin's day the owners were three actors who used The Bohemian Pirate as their day job. In those days you couldn't always get very good coffee in London, but The Bohemian Pirate had a real Italian coffee machine and Ronan knew how to use it. Ronan had a flair for the business; the idea of the café as a fall-back day job had been his, and then he got Keith and Fleur to go in with him. The three worked well together and could cover for each other when one of them had an audition. The Bohemian Pirate was closed in the evening, so even if one of them ever got cast in a long-running show they could still operate the café. They had a group of friends they could call on in case of emergencies or matinées. Swithin was on the fringe of their group (which was also mostly on the fringe) and stood in a time or two behind the counter. Everything seemed to interrupt his cogitations that summer.

That couldn't have been the reason he went off to America. I'm sure he has interruptions there, too. For someone who said he didn't like to be interrupted when he was working, Swithin almost invited it, although not intentionally. I suppose people would ask before they sat at his table. That's only polite. If they asked if Swithin minded if they sat there, he would look up as though startled and engaged in deep thought—as he probably was. He would give them a blank look and pause long enough to give them second thoughts about their request. But in the end he would relent. Sometimes there was something about those people, or about Swithin's work at the moment, that made him tolerate an interruption. I don't think he is as averse to interruptions as he claims, and anyway Swithin is too polite to be rude to anyone. I've never told him, but I think he gives off vibes—sympathetic-ear vibes or tell-me-all-about-it vibes.

Even before his book was a success, he got himself invited to lecture in different places and then within another year or two, there he was in California! He's in Chicago now. We keep in touch by email, but when he first went, hardly anyone outside universities had email. Swithin didn't even have a computer! He still wrote everything with a pen! But something seemed to change after that summer. Swithin seemed more self-confident somehow. He was always ambitious, but after that summer he had more of a sense of direction. He knew what he wanted.

We used to wonder if something had happened during that July and August—if one of those talkative visitors to The Bohemian Pirate had given him an idea or encouraged him in some way. I tried to think back over the stories he had told me. Were there ambitious, driven people who had given a boost to his own ambition? Were there failures who reminded him to go for it while he had the chance? Well, as Daddy always says when he can't make up his mind, the jury's still out.

THE EDITOR

Other members of staff at King Edward sometimes came into The Bohemian Pirate, too. They would nod to each other and sometimes sit at the same table, especially if they wanted to talk shop or if they had some juicy bit of gossip to share. Sometimes, like Swithin, they brought a book or some work with them and, like Swithin, they sat engrossed in it as they sipped their Lavazza or nibbled a Danish.

The staff and students at King Edward College in London University had to put up with the other colleges – and especially University College – calling it Potato College or even Spud-U-Like. At athletic contests there were predictable taunts about getting "mashed" and so on. When I was there myself – after Swithin had already left – I saw it first hand, but it only bonded us King Edward students all the closer. People from U.C. would spot our distinctive orange scarves and make cracks about potatoes or chips and so forth. It was very unoriginal. Their little wisecracks were handed down from generation to generation like some tatty old mascot. We didn't let it get to us.

One day when Swithin was sitting at his usual table that he imagined was inconspicuous, a colleague of his walked in and made straight for

4

him. I say "colleague", but J. Alexander Windley wasn't in his department. They were just on nodding terms. Windley was younger and had just started at KEC. Alexander Windley never liked to be called Alex. He was new and enthusiastic – not exactly about his subject but about his career. He had figured out how to get a step ahead of the competition – the competition being his colleagues in his own department and everyone else in any related field. Maybe that is why he chose Swithin to confide in, since their different fields put Swithin at a safe distance.

"Hi!" he said cheerily as he sat down at Swithin's table. "How's it going?"

But before Swithin could sum up for him how it was going, Alexander Windley started crowing about his new idea. Windley was a lecturer in the newly formed Department of Philology, Linguistics, and Usage Studies. It was apparently called "PLUS" by those in the know.

"Do you know any editors of scholarly journals?" Windley asked. Swithin began to think about it and was going to answer when Windley exclaimed, "If you didn't before, you do now! I've just founded a new journal! How do you think that will look on my c.v.!"

Swithin said it would look very good. "What's the name of your journal?"

"I have found an area of study which has not had a journal devoted to it until now. I put it to the Chair of PLUS and he managed to get funding for it. Of course, it will make the whole department look good, too, to have an international journal edited and published by them. In fact, it will reflect well on the whole College. And the whole university, too, of course. A ripple effect! I'm issuing a call for papers for the first issue! I've already had a couple, and a few suggestions and queries!"

"Well," said Swithin, "it sounds like you're on your way. I wish you the best of luck. But what exactly..."

"You know how important scholarly articles are! Important for the whole field and..." he lowered his voice to a confidential tone, "for your career. For your professional reputation!"

"Certainly research is very important in any area, and the publication of research. So tell me..."

"So the scholars in our area will have a new outlet for their research publications, and a new research tool! My journal will be quoted in all sorts of places. Footnotes, bibliographies!"

"And you'll be the editor. But what's it..."

"I thought I would put 'editor and founder' on the inside cover. You know, where I say where to send contributions in how many copies, floppy and hardcopy and all that. Or maybe 'founder and editor'. What do you think?"

"Well," said Swithin, "you founded it before you edited it, but what is the title of this new journal?"

"The title! Didn't I tell you the title?"

"No."

"Oh well, in that case. It's to be devoted to the study of abbreviations, mainly in English, but also in other languages, and the title is Abbrev. Witty, eh?"

"Very witty."

"Abbrev.! That says it all, doesn't it? Better than these long-winded titles that have to be shortened. Think of the Journal of English and Germanic Philology! It's usually called JEGP. Or like PMLA, you know. That stands for Publications of the Modern Language Association, but that was such a mouthful that they changed it officially to just PMLA!"

"Abbrev.," said Swithin. "Yes, that has something. Like..." Swithin said the first thing that popped into his mind, because it had been in the news recently, "like NATO

"No," said Windley, "that's an acronym. That's different."

"It doesn't fall within your brief as an abbreviation?"

"No. Anyway, there's already a scholarly journal devoted to acronyms."

"There is?"

"Yes, that's 'Jo-eena', spelled J-O-E-N-A, the Journal of Established and New Acronyms. That's been around for a good few years."

"So there was a need for this journal of abbreviations, and you decided to fill it. Well done!"

"The need was there for all to see, actually, but I was the one who acted on it. You notice nobody at UC thought of it! Nobody in any of the other London colleges!" Windley could hardly open his mouth without sounding pleased with himself, but Swithin didn't hold it against him. It was apparently true: scholars in a certain specialised field had been crying out (in a restrained and decorous way) for exactly the journal that Windley had founded and was now editing. The cracks between the various scholarly areas were becoming harder to find, but Windley had succeeded. He had seen an opportunity at the right time. People would send him their articles and other people would read them in his journal and quote them in their own articles, and so on ad infinitum. Or ad infin.

Swithin wasn't exactly envious, but he noticed that Windley had seen a chance for advancement and had seized it. I wonder if he thought life was passing him by or something like that. It wasn't really, as far as we could see, but it's very subjective, isn't it, whether life is passing you by? At any rate, by the next summer he was in L.A. and anyone wandering into The Bohemian Pirate would have to look elsewhere for an empty ear to fill with his story.

"There will be a copy of Abbrev. in the College library, of course," said Windley. "You could have a look at it. You might like to see what we're doing in the field."

"Are you offering a course in the subject?" Swithin asked politely.

"Maybe next term. We've been talking about it. We haven't yet gone into it fully, but a course is in the cards. I'm putting some material together now. It might be a component in another related course. I'm working on it."

"So it might not take up a whole term?" Swithin said.

"We'll have to see how the course material goes together."

"You might offer a shortened course in abbreviations?" Swithin enquired innocently.

"Yes," replied Windley, but even as the word left his lips he suspected that Swithin was somehow making fun of him. He wondered if Swithin was taking the new journal as seriously as it deserved. Of course, later Swithin would appreciate its importance. He would see how the whole College would go up in the world as a result of Abbrev. When he, Windley, was a reader or even a professor and Swithin was still a footling lecturer, they would see who had the last laugh! In the meantime, Windley felt somehow got at. As his triumphant vindication was still in the future, he didn't have a good answer for Swithin's possible mickey-taking.

"Oh!" said Windley, "is that the time? Better get back to work! Well, it was good to run into you here. See you later." He sprang up, jostling the table a little as he did so.

"Right," said Swithin, "Bye, Wind." And Windley had hurried off so precipitously that he couldn't be sure whether or not he had heard both syllables of his name.

THE RENDEZVOUS

My brother Swithin got quite a lot done, he used to say, sitting at his table at The Bohemian Pirate. Swithin needed to be near his room at the College and the department office to collect his mail and make phone calls. The secretaries in the office just had to put up with all the noise and dust that summer. Swithin would escape to The Bohemian Pirate and chat with Ronan and Keith and sometimes with Fleur if she was around. The Bohemian Pirate was what they fell back on when they weren't in a play, and they seemed to spend a lot of time falling back on it. Once or twice they even asked Swithin to lend a hand when one of them went for an audition. They had a running joke that Swithin was their understudy. He learned to make very professional cappuccino that summer, so if he stops being a lecturer he can fall back in the cappuccino himself, so to speak. But that's not very likely since he's in Chicago now making a name for himself, and not as a coffee maker.

One day that summer — it was a Monday morning and Swithin had finished his chores at the College and had walked round to The Bohemian Pirate – he was sitting at his usual table when a middle-aged woman walked in, looking a little lost. She went to the counter and asked Keith, "Excuse me, please. Could you direct me to the nearest Tube?" She spoke with an American accent.

Keith was about the last person you should ask for directions anywhere. He travelled by bus whenever possible and was surprisingly vague about the whole Underground. Swithin looked up, fatally, and saw the forlorn look in the woman's eyes. He got up and went to the door with her and pointed toward the street, explaining all the time, then he gestured how she should turn to the left and then the next right. Instead of going off in the direction he had shown her, however, she followed him back into the café and sat down opposite him at his table.

"I think it's the Northern Line, as I recall," she said. "Tottingham Road, something like that. Tottingham Park Road?"

"Tottenham Court Road?" Swithin suggested.

"That's it!" she said. "Tottenham Court Road. It's the station for the British Museum."

Swithin nodded.

"Although the station for my hotel was the next one, Goodge Street. I was a student then – it was years ago – and travelling with another girl. It was the summer of 1966. I'd just spend a year at the Sorbonne. I did my junior year abroad. Nowadays the young people go everywhere and there are junior-year-abroad programmes all over Europe, South America, China – amazing places. It's wonderful for them. Thirty years ago we went to Paris, and that was about it. I was lucky to get to

11

go. I was the only one in our French department who went that year."

"We have a few American junior-year students at my college," Swithin said. "King Edward College." And he gestured in the direction of the College, the opposite direction from the Tube station. "Part of the University of London. We get the brightest students because they're the only ones who can find it." It was an old joke but the American hadn't heard it before and laughed.

"Well, I can believe that!" she said. "I tried to take a bus, but I couldn't tell where it was going and once you get on it, there's nothing to tell you where you are or where you're headed. Not like the ones in Paris. They're easy – a child could take them and get around Paris, but here you have to know the city first. I got off the bus when I realized I was lost and was only going to get 'loster'." She smiled for the first time.

Swithin was thinking that it was only Monday and he had all the rest of the week to work on his book.

"So you haven't been back to London since your student days?" Swithin enquired.

"No," she said, "not since that summer of 1966. Things have changed so much! But that's true everywhere, isn't it? It's certainly true of St. Louis, so I guess it's true in Europe, too. I came over on a ferry from Dieppe and then by train to Waterloo Station. The taxi cabs drove right into the station – right up to the track where you got off the train! I was travelling with a friend from our group in Paris and we took one of those big black taxis to this hotel on Gower Street. I see the cabs are still just the same, but now they're other colours, too. The hotel was called the Russell House Hotel. It made us smile, because the name reminded us of the Parker House in Chicago, but it was just a row house and it had eight or ten rooms. Our room had a fireplace in it, I remember. We thought that was so quaint."

Swithin was rather taken with her American accent and her appearance, too. She was in her early 50s and was dressed smartly, but not overdressed. Her hair was short and wavy and still a dark natural blonde. He could sense her nostalgia. It was odd to hear foreigners talk about your home city. He found her story interesting, and now she took him into her confidence.

"You see, there was this boy in Paris. I can look back on it now... We were falling in love. He was German, an absolutely charming, good-looking fellow. Don't get me wrong. I've been happily married to someone else for 27 years. This is all water under the bridge. We were in a class together and got acquainted. It was one of those irresistible attractions. We wanted to be together all the time. The end of the year came. We were both going to be in London that July, the end of July. We decided to meet and have one last day together. We were going to decide whether we could be together more permanently. It was a big decision and would have presented problems for both of us. It's just as well....

"His name was Helmut. Helmut... He had dark hair and a lovely smile. Wonderful sense of humour. He was a good dancer. Helmut was going to London a week before I was, and going home earlier, but there were two or three days when our stays overlapped. Helmut suggested we meet at the British Museum, since that was such a landmark.

"I was glad to find out that the Russell House was actually quite close to the British Museum. I could walk down there easily. It was only about four or five blocks away. Helmut had said, 'Let's meet there at noon next Thursday.' *Le jeudi prochain*. We agreed to meet at the front entrance at noon on Thursday.

"I saw where it was. The big lions were a real landmark, all right. I went in one day. I remember a huge room full of Chinese porcelain and bronze horses and pots. I was glad to know where it was so that I could meet Helmut there the next day."

"The lions..." Swithin started to say, but she went on.

"Yes. The next day my friend Rachel went off to do some shopping and I went in good time to the entrance of the British Museum to meet Helmut. I got there early and didn't mind waiting. You know, it could have been a very momentous day for me. We might have gotten engaged. My future could have been entirely different if we had decided to let this relationship be more than just a passing student romance. Helmut was a remarkable young man – honest, intelligent, fun to be with. Still, it might not have worked out. We both might have regretted it. Maybe it was all for the best. If I had married Helmut, I would never have known Jack, never have had my children. And then, where would we have lived? Would I have been living in Germany all these years? Or would Helmut have been happy in St. Louis or wherever we ended up?

"So I got to the British Museum, as planned, and waited, full of anticipation and excitement. It got to be 12 noon and I started looking at all the passers-by, because very soon one of them would be him. Helmut was very rarely late for anything, and if he said he would meet you at a certain place you could depend on it. That was another nice thing about him. It got to be a quarter past, and he still hadn't come, but in a big city you can get held up, and I didn't know how far he was coming from. Then it was 12:30 and still no Helmut. Now I was getting worried. I waited until 1:30. I waited for an hour and a half and I couldn't believe what I was doing. This wasn't the plan at all! I had thought of various ways the day might turn out, but I had never thought of this – of the possibility that the day wouldn't happen at all.

"I went back to the hotel room. I was thunderstruck. I was terribly worried that something had happened to Helmut. He would never have stood me up. Even if he intended to break it off with me, even if he was planning to say it was all over, he would never have done it this way. He was a very honourable young man. I didn't know what to think. I didn't have any other plans for the day and Rachel wouldn't be back until the stores closed. I hadn't thought about the course of the day beyond thinking that it would be with Helmut and that it didn't matter in the least what exactly we decided to do, because we were going to be together.

"Even before I got to the hotel – before I left the British Museum – I realized that I didn't know how to contact Helmut. Not then or ever. I didn't know where he was staying in London and I didn't even know his home address. We'd been so wrapped up with each other in Paris that we hadn't bothered to exchange home addresses and of course I didn't know my college address yet for the next year. We were going to see each other again so it hadn't been important to do that kind of thing yet. I suppose we would have remembered to do it on that Thursday when we met at the British Museum. When you're a student, your address changes so often. If your parents move, too, you can completely lose track of people. But I hadn't even given him my parents' address and I didn't have his."

"Those lions..." Swithin said again. "They're in Montague Place."

"I found that out. That's the street in back of the British Museum, isn't it?"

"Yes," said Swithin. "The front entrance is in Great Russell Street."

"On that Friday I was still devastated by what had happened, but the next day I was walking around in that area and I went around to the other side of the Museum and found the front entrance. Helmut had been to London before and of course knew where the front of it was. It's much, much bigger than the back entrance, with all those steps and pillars and the whole forecourt, but if you've only seen the back, it looks like the front of anything else. I mean, the lions are exactly like the lions out in front of the New York Public Library. Lions are usually at the front of things, aren't they? You don't expect lions to be at the back door."

Swithin found the whole story terribly sad, although the woman sitting across from him didn't seem exactly sad.

"It has its ridiculous side, of course," she said, smiling. "But at the time... At the time it was devastating. And I could only guess what had happened. He'd been waiting at the front while I was standing around at the back. We had had just that big building between us, between us and our possible future together. And there we were, standing around looking at our watches and waiting for the other to come. On that Saturday when I realized what had happened I even went to the entrance—the the right entrance—and waited for a while. I knew I was two days late, but I somehow thought he might have come back or he might happen to be there and I might see him. Isn't that crazy? At least I realized that he was probably all right and hadn't been run over by a taxi. Then I realized what he must think of me! And there would never be any way to explain to him what had happened. I wonder if it ever occurred to him that I had gone to the wrong place, or did he think that something terrible had happened to me or that I was too cowardly to meet him for the last time?"

"That's a very sad story," Swithin said. "Can I buy you a cup of coffee?"

"It is sad, isn't it?" It's sad because there is nothing, absolutely nothing, that I can ever do about it. Yes, thank you. I'd like a cappuccino."

Swithin gestured to Ronan behind the counter and asked for two cappuccinos.

"This is a nice little place," the woman said. "I wonder if it was here in 1966. But then I wasn't in this part of town then, I don't think."

"No," said Swithin, "I think it's newer than that. It opened only a few years ago. Three or four years ago. I don't know what was here before. I've been lecturing at King Edward for three years."

"Lecturing?" she said. "Like teaching? Like being a professor?"

"Teaching, yes. I'm not a professor yet! That takes years!" Swithin smiled, because he knew that Americans thought that everyone who lectured was a professor.

"I wonder what Helmut finally did," she said as the cappuccinos arrived. "He might be a professor of French somewhere in Germany now. Europe is so small. He could be in another country, too. Still, a German teaching French...he probably stayed in Germany. But maybe he didn't end up teaching French, after all. He was very intelligent. He could have gone into business, or maybe diplomacy. He could have used French in a job like either of those. I'll never know, will I?"

"No," said Swithin regretfully. "It doesn't look like it. I'm sorry."

"Don't be!" she exclaimed. "Don't worry about it. I'm only thinking about it now because I'm here. I told Jack about it, and he thought it was a pretty crazy story. It makes me think of those lines by John Greenleaf Whittier in "Maud Muller". Do you know that poem? Maybe not, it's such an American classic. 'Of all the words of tongue and pen, / The saddest are these: "It might have been'.'"

That seemed to strike a chord with Swithin. "'Of all the words of...'"

"'Of tongue and pen,'" the American supplied, "'The saddest are these: "It might have been.'""

Swithin now repeated the couplet to the woman's satisfaction.

"That's it!" she said. That's from "Maud Muller" by John Greenleaf Whittier. Maud Muller is a farm girl raking the hay and a man on horseback stops and asks her for a cup of water. If something had come of it, she might have become the wife of a judge instead of staying a poor farm woman. But nothing came of it."

"Ah, yes," said Swithin. "What might have been."

"You just never know, do you? Helmut must be married now, too, with children and maybe grandchildren. What a thought! Golly! Still and all, it would be nice to see him just once more, just to see what he was doing now. Just to see how he turned out. You know?"

"Yes," Swithin said. "That would be nice." They sipped their cappuccino together and Swithin thought of the young couple all those years ago and their missed opportunity and the impossibility of ever going back and making amends. They each had the memory of the non-meeting, and what was Helmut telling his friends over cappuccino now somewhere in Germany? "Once I knew an

American girl in Paris..." Swithin looked across at the American woman from St. Louis, smartly dressed, a tourist visiting London. "Well," he said, "don't let it put you off the British Museum. Have you seen the Rosetta Stone? There are some splendid things there."

"Perhaps I will go and see what's inside," she said, smiling a little ruefully. "I don't know what's in it, except for those Chinese pots."

"The Rosetta Stone is on the Great Russell Street side of the Museum," Swithin said, and added, "but you can get there from either entrance."

MONOPOLY

All that summer when they were rewiring Swithin's building—rewiring and all the rest of it— he would sit working at his table in the café. Swithin, who was always an optimist, thought that he would be out of the way there and nobody would go near him. He was drafting his first book then, writing by hand in a notebook or on a clipboard. Sometimes he had a box of file cards with him on the table. He thought any normal person would see that he was busy, but he lived to learn that The Bohemian Pirate was full of, and seemed to attract, people who weren't that normal.

The little man who came and sat across from him had a furtive look and kept glancing toward the door. "What now?" Swithin wondered.

A colleague of Swithin's had just written a book about the fall of the Berlin Wall and the recent political changes in Eastern Europe. Swithin had a copy with him, lying on the table. The stranger lit up when he saw it.

"You are reading about this Wall?" he asked in a hard-to-place accent.

"Yes," said Swithin looking up, because he couldn't help being polite.

"Ah, the Wall!" said the man. "That said it all, didn't it? They had to lock people in, like a jail. And if you tried to get out of that jail, they would put you in another smaller jail!" he laughed with more hilarity than the joke warranted. "You had to go straight to jail without passing Go!" He thought this was exceptionally funny, too.

"Yes," said Swithin, my polite brother. "Are you from that part of the world yourself?"

There followed a family genealogy that was bewildering. The man, whose name was Jozef, had been born in Hungary of Polish and Czech parents, or the other way around, but it seemed that his first language was German, closely followed by Czech, Polish, Hungarian, Ukrainian, Russian and Yiddish. Have I missed one out? Did I say Polish? Yes. There may have been another one. And English of course. His English was quite good.

The point was that he had been a Hungarian refugee in 1956 when there was a major uprising there and most of Jozef's family had been killed or imprisoned. He had hated the regime before, but now he felt a deep personal revulsion towards it.

Swithin offered sympathy in retrospect.

"But I had a plan, you see," Jozef said. "I found a way to fight back. I gradually formed a group of like-minded persons. We discovered each other through certain émigré channels. I was living in Vienna then. Later on I was in Paris, and all the time I was organising and planning. We needed to do something, you see. It is not good to feel that there is nothing you can do."

Swithin couldn't help it. He asked, "And what was your plan?"

"Ah!" exclaimed Jozef. "My plan! Our plan, because I had a cousin who thought of it first. Then I worked on it and refined it. Then we brought in other people. We had some graphic designers, people like that. Oh, we gathered quite a group over the years." He smiled to himself and then seemed to realise that he hadn't answered Swithin's question. "We did a bit of smuggling," he said finally.

"What did you smuggle?" Swithin asked in spite of himself.

"We smuggled certain games," he said, lowering his voice and glancing around the café.

"Games?" said Swithin. "Like tiddly-winks? Snakes and Ladders?"

"Snakes and ladders," the refugee said, considering the possibilities. "No. Monopoly."

"You smuggled Monopoly games?"

"Yes, but first we had to adapt them. We smuggled them to different places, you see, so we had to adapt them."

Swithin was thoroughly puzzled by this time, and even a little curious. "How did you adapt them and what was the point of smuggling them?"

"Well," said Jozef as though everything that was to follow was entirely self evident. "First of all, the Monopoly games we could find in those days were either English or American. The English ones all related to London, you know—fair enough if you're English—and the American ones all have to do with some seaside town in the States. So you see if we were going to get them into, let us say, Brno for example, or Upper Silesia, or Budapest, or... but you see what I mean. As time went on we had quite a large operation. We got to all those places in the end, and more." He smiled with satisfaction.

Swithin was still puzzled, though. "But why bother to smuggle these..."

"They were forbidden, of course!" Jozef exclaimed. "Don't you see? In those days practically anything from the West was contraband! You could never keep track of everything that was contraband. One day something would be all right, and the next day it would be strictly forbidden. Even the authorities could never be sure, so they confiscated things just to be on the safe side. You can't imagine!"

And very likely Swithin couldn't. He had never had anything confiscated since the day he took a catapult to school, aged ten.

"Monopoly," the Hungarian/Czech/Pole said, realising he would have to explain things in simple terms to this Englishman, "Monopoly, you see, is about capitalism, about having money, buying property and getting rich. Communism, you remember, was about poverty and everyone being equally poor." You could sense how much Jozef relished using the past tense here. "Try to imagine the thrill of owning railways in those conditions. Imagine the thrill of putting a hotel on Wenceslas Square, for example, and growing rich from the rent! Of course, the official line was that this was a terrible thing, this owning of property and charging

rent and growing rich, just unspeakably terrible."
Josef laughed again. "Utterly terrible, you see."

"Ah," said Swithin, "so that was one in the eye for
the authorities, was it, when you introduced these
games into their territory?"

"One in the eye, yes, exactly. And furthermore it
inspired people. They saw what they were missing
and they knew how corrupt their rulers were and
that the system they lived under was much worse
than simply not owning a hotel on Wenceslas
Square. Monopoly was simpler than real life, too,
because there is no black market in Monopoly. The
system they lived under had certain advantages, it
is true, but on the whole it was better to be in the
West and run the risk of going bankrupt than to be
in the East and not have anything to buy with your
play money." He chortled again. "It was Monopoly
money anyway, but without the game to go with it!"

The man Jozef was getting positively aerated with
the memory of it all, and so Swithin brought him
back down to earth. "So you smuggled these
games, but first you had to produce them—to have
something to smuggle—in the first place?"

"Oh yes. We got people to design them. Very
hush-hush. We should have paid the Parker
Brothers Company royalties or some sort of
payment to adapt their game, but we didn't. We
were illegal on all fronts! We were trying to
undermine communist regimes by exposing them
to the fun of capitalism, but we were also flouting
capitalism by pirating the game in the first place!"

"But," said Swithin, "mightn't those same
regimes have said, 'By all means bring in those

games of Monopoly so that our people can see what a dog-eat-dog affair capitalism is'—because the game is quite 'unregulated' unlike the real thing?"

"Yes, you might think they would see it that way, but they didn't. Oh yes, it illustrated the bad side of capitalism. But they didn't want their people to realise the excitement of having money and watching it increase. Either that or they weren't sure what to do about it so they banned it anyway, just in case. When they were in any doubt, you see, they erred on the side of forbidding things. If you failed to ban a thing, you could get into trouble—maybe months or years later—for being too lax, whereas there were few penalties for being too strict. So better to be safe than sorry."

"How did you go about smuggling these Monopoly boards and so forth?" Swithin asked, thinking of the bulky box our Monopoly set at home lived in, imagining it being challenged at various fortified borders in the old East Bloc. Unsmiling guards with machine guns and police dogs would find the boxes and scowl and demand bribes. Swithin was getting into the mood of the thing.

"There are several elements to the game," Jozef answered. "The counters, the cards, the little wooden houses and hotels, the paper money, a pair of dice, and finally the board. The small pieces were very easy to carry in different places—we often made those little metal counters into a charm bracelet—and the board was printed on a large handkerchief or scarf. All those things were easy to carry in a way that aroused no suspicion. Erik always wore a Monopoly board in his breast pocket, for example, with only the white corners showing. No one guessed that it contained Unter den Linden or Hungarian railways or that kind of thing. We were never caught! We were playing a game with a game!" He laughed a little hysterically and then lowered his voice. "We were never caught," he repeated.

"That's very good," Swithin said. "What would have happened if you had been caught?"

"Who knows? Maybe nothing. Maybe a lot. It could have been very serious in different places at different times." He lowered his voice again. "It could have been very serious indeed in the wrong place at the wrong time. They would have called it 'undermining the Revolution' or something like that. That could have been very serious if they had understood what we were up to!"

"But they never did," said Swithin politely.

"No. It was all worth it, you know. We had our problems, but it was all worth it. Oh yes, in the beginning there were plenty of problems! Organising things, getting everything together. Getting everybody to agree. We had such discussions! Choosing the cities! You see, everyone had his favourite city. Some we could agree on easily. Berlin. Budapest. You might think Warsaw would be an obvious choice, but the street names had all been changed and some of the streets were gone. They had been wiped off the map. It was hard to put hotels on non-existent streets and expect people to pay rent for them. It was hard for people to imagine having great wealth based on

27

such poverty and ruin. Monopoly is a fantasy, of course, naturally, but there are limits to it. We tried Gdansk, we tried Kraków. We even tried Wrocław. There was a little more left of some of those places."

"I see the problem," Swithin murmured.

"And the Czechoslovakians couldn't agree! They were split between Prague and Bratislava. In the end we had to make up two sets, one for each place. And then later Brno. Oh, we had a set for Vilnius in Lithuania and Lvóv in the Ukraine. People all over the Bloc would meet in secret and revel in high finance. They spent their days helping their country pretend to have 'full employment' even if they had nothing to do—or else did really hard work with obsolete equipment—and then they spent their evenings charging rent for their property and buying and selling railways! I think we brought pleasure and hope to many people."

"Or could it have made them more unhappy, if they thought they'd never get to do any of that in reality?"

"We always felt we were showing them the excitement that comes from managing money— from having money to manage in the first place. And don't forget: they knew they were doing something risky. They knew that their game of Monopoly with friends with the door locked was a small act of rebellion. It was also a steam valve. It helped them get through their days. They would spend hours in a queue to buy some ordinary commodity—cheese or pencils or toilet paper, you name it—and they could think, 'Ah, but tonight I will buy the Trans-Siberian Express!' When I look back on it, it gave us great pleasure to do that for people."

"I see," said Swithin. "Did you get any feedback about it? Was anybody punished for playing Monopoly behind the Iron Curtain as was?"

"Not as far as I know. No, I think our operation carried relatively little risk for our customers. Our clients. If they heard someone coming they could quickly replace the evidence of a Monopoly game with a chess set. Some people kept a half-played game of chess permanently on their chessboard so that they could pretend to be engrossed in it if there was an unexpected knock at the door."

"The Russians have always been famous for their love of chess," Swithin said.

"Exactly! How do we know they were always playing chess? Then too, the satellite countries were supposed to emulate the Soviet Union in all ways possible, so it would have been an entirely good thing to be 'caught' playing chess!"

"So it worked both ways," Swithin said. "They were being rebellious, but at the same time they could look very supportive of the new Soviet order. Very clever."

"Yes, very clever. We thought it was very clever, too. But it was all a secret. No one will ever know the whole story. Even I, even I do not know the whole story. The set-backs, the triumphs. Janos and his handkerchiefs. Magda's collection of charm bracelets. The way we adapted the board in Czech and Hungarian and Polish... It is a rather exciting story," he added soberly. "It would make an interesting story—as interesting in its way as that one about the Wall." He nodded toward the book on the table, *The* Crumbling *of the Berlin Wall* by Swithin's colleague.

"I daresay it would," said Swithin. "I know this man—the author. I'll mention it to him."

Jozef brightened a bit. "That would be nice," he said. "Still, no one will ever know the whole story."

"No, I suppose not," said Swithin, "but you could write your part of it. You could write down what you yourself know."

Josef looked at Swithin and then glanced around the café. "Write it down. Yes! I believe I will! I'll write the whole thing down! Everything I know! I'll write the story from my point of view, from the beginning! And may I show you the results, the instalments as I go along?"

Swithin wasn't expecting this. "Well, I... I'm quite busy myself. I'm writing this book..." he gestured to his clipboard with a blank sheet of paper on it. Jozef was looking a little chopfallen. "Yes, of course I'll look at it," Swithin said, hoping that the electricians would finish with his college room soon.

MALCOLM

My brother Swithin used to say that he had only to look up from his table at The Bohemian Pirate to see something or someone remarkable. One day he was sipping his cappuccino and pondering the transition from one chapter to another, when he looked up and saw, not one of the usual students or locals or even off-piste shoppers, but a rather frail-looking old lady. She was wearing a long skirt and a generally old-fashioned looking outfit. It had once been quite smart-looking, in a Victoria and Albert Museum kind of way. She was even wearing gloves and a hat with a little veil.

The old lady went to the counter and asked for Assam tea and a piece of apple strudel. Ronan invited her to sit down and said he would bring it to her table. Swithin was so overcome by her appearance and her apparent frailty that he did an unprecedented thing. He stood up and asked her to join him! My brother Swithin! Swithin was always trying to keep his table to himself. "Thank you, young man. That is very kind of you. I have been on my feet rather a lot today."

When she sat down Swithin saw that she was not as frail as he had first thought, although she was certainly very elderly. She had an old-fashioned dignified air about her.

Swithin wondered if she was lost, because people who wandered into The Bohemian Pirate were either connected with King Edward College or had business in the area or were lost. However, Swithin could not bring himself to ask such a presumptuous question. Instead he asked if she was connected with King Edward College.

"Oh no," she said. "Although I remember when it was quite a new college. I don't recall that I knew many students there, but I knew of the college." Ronan brought the tea and strudel to the table and set them down respectfully in front of the old lady. She nodded to him in a way that could have meant "thank you" or "that will be all".

"You know, young man," she said to Swithin, "sitting here like this with you reminds me of another young man I once had tea and cake with. You aren't Scottish, are you?"

"No," Swithin said. "I'm English. A Londoner. Born and bred."

The old lady set her cup back onto the saucer. The cup and saucer were heavy restaurant ware, and Swithin thought that she must have been more used to drinking out of fine china, probably with flowers on. She looked at him and then gazed off to one side and slightly above him. When she began to speak Swithin found that he couldn't take his eyes off her. Her voice had an old-fashioned well-bred timbre and she spoke clearly and softly. Swithin felt that he was hearing English as it had not been spoken for years. Her accent had a pre-war, Bright-Young-Thing, Mitford-sisters flavour. He didn't say a word, even when she paused, because interrupting her would feel like interrupting the Queen.

"He was up at Balliol with my brother. He was a simply fabulous dancer! One simply wafted about the dance floor. One simply forgot one had feet. We were lucky in a way. Most of the boys our age were too young to have been in the Great War. By the time I was of age we were all living life to the full. We used to go up to Malcolm's home, a great castle in Scotland called Craig Dhu that the Hatton-Grants had owned more or less forever. Malcolm's mother was Canadian and a bluestocking and took up Gaelic, but be that as it may, she was a fine woman — her hair was completely white when I knew her. She wanted to rename the place Sgian Buie for some reason, but Sir Robert finally got her off the notion.

"Now, Craig Dhu was a quite marvellous old pile dating from sometime in the Middle Ages or thereabouts. You could never get a straight answer out of any of them about it. You'd casually mention the subject at dinner, or later over coffee, and they would talk about it for hours, but you'd never get a proper answer. It was built during this reign, no it was that reign, or it had been slept in by various kings and queens while they were all still Scottish, if you see what I mean. Alexanders and Roberts and Davids and Jameses with low numbers. Malcolm always said he thought the oldest bits dated from the 1260s — now he at least had a definite opinion and he was reading history so perhaps he knew.

"Malcolm was such a kind young man, very thoughtful, sweet, he would notice if you were sitting in a draught or had an empty glass or anything like that. We girls were all fond of him — not that it did us any good, you know dear, because it was only other young men who could steal his heart. We all knew that and we took it in our stride. Everyone seems so obsessed with that sort of thing nowadays. Of course, it was illegal, I suppose. But I don't recall any policemen at those house parties, except when we had fancy dress, but that hardly counts. The boys were all right as long as they didn't do foolish things in public under some policeman's nose.

"Malcolm invited a whole group of us up for a week in June, I believe it was, in about 1925 or perhaps a bit later. We all went up from King's Cross on the train, and that was a house party in itself! A train party. What fun we had! Nowadays people would motor up or even fly and it wouldn't be the same. We simply took over the dining car, you know, and we had champagne and perhaps oysters, or I may be thinking of another time. Even the ones who hadn't known each other in London were old friends by the time we got to Inverness and changed trains for this village near Craig Dhu. At the village we were met by several motors and ferried off to the castle.

"Now, this castle. I've said it was quite old. It was high up on a great dark outcrop. You came round a corner from one glen up and over into the next one, and there was the huge outcrop in the distance with all the towers and turrets. It was a sight to see! If it was the first time people had seen it they would all stop talking and there would be a sort of gasp go up from them. The car would go all quiet and then this gasp. You could count on it, you would know it was coming. We would finally get there, down to the floor of the glen, part way round the loch, then up a steep winding drive through the trees and through the gates and then further up and then you would come out right in front of the castle in a big gravelled area with the garden away to the right behind a wall. It would still be light. In June it was always light.

"Malcolm used to say the place was haunted, and no one doubted him for an instant. We would have doubted him if he'd said it wasn't. There were supposed to be two ghosts, I recall, the main ghost and a lesser one — I mean one that didn't put in so many appearances. Or perhaps three. The one was a lady dressed in white with a tartan sash (or maybe I've invented the sash, maybe she was just white) and she was very sad, she did nothing but weep. I never heard or saw her myself, but I knew several people who said they'd heard her at night weeping and sobbing in a certain corridor upstairs. She was seen in the garden too, sitting by an old fountain with her head in her hands, weeping. I know Malcolm used to feel terribly sorry for her, but I don't know how you can make a ghost happy. You know, dear, if they're upset about something that happened in 1512 or whenever, there's not a great deal you can do for them.

"But Malcolm wanted to help and was always hoping to talk to her. Can you imagine? But that was just like Malcolm, you know. He couldn't bear to see anybody unhappy or upset.

"He was such a sweet boy. One could talk to him. He was quite manly, he was well-built and athletic. He played rugger and rowed. I mean as in rowed a boat not rode a horse, but in fact he rode well, too, rode a horse, I mean. So he could hold his own with the hearties, you see, but then he also had this lovely sensitive side, too.

"Now, the other one I mentioned. He was a great hulking thing in a sort of leather waistcoat. Sometimes he carried a targe and claymore about with him. I saw him once. It was quite strange. I suppose it has its amusing aspect. He was evidently someone called Roderick. My sister Edith and I were put in a lovely room with a rather splendid bathroom overlooking the garden. We had quantities of mirrors and a tub with a mahogany surround. That was long before everyone got so excited about mahogany, we just thought it looked nice. One morning just as I was running the bath this large, rather hairy, person clad in leather breeches and a sleeveless jacket appeared. I was about to take off my dressing gown when there he was in the doorway! My first thought was that it was perfectly outrageous to have uncouth-looking strangers barging into one's bathroom, well, into one's bedroom, too, actually, because they were adjoining. So I faced him and said very clearly, 'Please leave this bathroom at once'. I said it in quite a forceful way, because I did not want this man to be in any doubt about whether I wanted his company. That was the first time I had ever seen a ghost. The message, as they say, got through, because he disappeared, faded like something you've bleached by mistake, just, you know, stopped being there. So that was Roderick.

"Malcolm had seen him many a time and oft. Malcolm, I believe, was a bit nervous about him. Indeed, quite nervous. He told my husband Andrew once that Roderick had bothered him a few times. He said 'bothered'. I had the impression at the time that, this Roderick was...was importuning him, was...well, flirting, as it were, in a way, with Malcolm. Malcolm thought it was funny at first, but then he found it rather a nuisance, as one would. I mean, this great hulking person with his beard. I believe he had a sort of hat as well. Yes, a kind of beret with a long pheasant feather in it. I remember it now. You cannot imagine what it looked like in that bathroom with all the mirrors, not that you could see Roderick in them. Malcolm rather dreaded these visits. I said to Malcolm once that he should just be firm with this Roderick person. He should simply tell him to leave, and mean it. You know, I think Malcolm would have been too kind-hearted to speak that way to anyone, dead or alive or whatever. He wouldn't have wanted to hurt anyone's feelings. Now, I didn't mind, you know. When I found him in my bathroom, I didn't care if I hurt his feelings. The truth is that I simply did not care tuppence about his feelings, but Malcolm would have been different, he would have thought how it would sound and how the other chap would take it. So I really don't know what he said. He would have said, 'My dear fellow, this

37

won't do, you know. You really ought to stop these appearances, don't you know. Now, if you don't mind, won't you please go away? There's a good fellow.' Malcolm would have been hopeless in dealing with the whole thing. I had a nanny once who was like that. She didn't last long. The next one, now that I think of it, is where I got the tone of voice I used in my encounter with Roderick. Yes, that's where I learned it, she would have dealt with him in very short order. She could have exorcised him with one look. If only it could have been that easy. It's a pity I didn't think of it at the time. I could have lent her to Malcolm and that would have been the end of it. I shouldn't joke about it though. It wasn't at all funny as time went on.

"I lost track of Malcolm for a while. Andrew and I were married and went out to Kenya for a few years and when we came back we seemed to take up with different people. I never went back to Craig Dhu, but I did see Malcolm once in London. I was in Fortnum's one day and he was there and we had tea together. We caught up with each other and I told him about Kenya and how we were back, and he told me about his life. His parents had died and he had inherited Craig Dhu but didn't live there. It was partly because of this Roderick. Roderick had become rather vicious and had threatened Malcolm with his claymore. We sat there in Fortnum's tearoom and he told me, rather sadly, how this ghost had become the bane of his existence. I'm not surprised he was violent, he looked the type. He would flail about with the claymore and knock things over and slice the curtains. Malcolm tried to talk to him, of course. Comfort him, I suppose, get him to talk about his problems. He must have had problems. Malcolm was so kind, so very kind, so gentle. There, I didn't mean to cry. I have a tissue. Oh dear, I'm as bad as the lady in the white gown at Craig Dhu! We never did find out what the matter was with her.

"But I believe I mentioned that there are three ghosts at Craig Dhu. Roderick hacked at him one night with his claymore and killed him while we were in Kenya. The third ghost was Malcolm."

Swithin stared at her as she dabbed at her eyes, raising the little half veil on her hat with the other hand. Fortunately she didn't notice that he was staring. Finally he said the only thing he could think of. "May I get you another cup of tea? Assam, wasn't it?" And she smiled and nodded.

ICE CREAM

My brother Swithin was so fond of everything Italian that it was no wonder that he heard the newcomer in The Bohemian Pirate who was ordering a latte at the counter. He didn't have an Italian accent, but he heard Keith call him Rocco. Rocco! For Swithin it said warm black olives and red tile roofs. Swithin used to start a lot of sentences with "When I was in Italy..." or even "When I used to live in Italy..." It was only a year and a half, but it was an important time for him.

The stranger inevitably sat down at Swithin's table in spite of all the evidence that he was in the middle of a working lunch (to say nothing of a working-all-morning-and-most-of-the-afternoon, since he had more or less moved his headquarters to The Bohemian Pirate while they were redecorating at King Edward College). But for once Swithin began a conversation with an interloper at his table.

"Did I hear Keith call you Rocco?" he asked.

"Yes," beamed the stranger. "Rocco Ritornelli. How do you do?" He half-rose from the seat he had just sat down on and offered his hand.

Swithin loved shaking hands with Italians. He loved the sense of ritual, the grave formality. He sprang up and seized Rocco by the hand. "Buon giorno!" he exclaimed.

"I don't speak Italian," said Rocco. "I understand it. I used to speak it with my grandparents when I was little. Then I forgot it. Sometimes I think of going to Italy and trying to get it back, but" – he shrugged – "you get busy, you get involved with other things." He took a sip of coffee, which was still too hot. "You get busy with your life and the years go by."

He spoke with the wisdom of old age, but he was younger than Swithin, who would have been about 30 then.

"It's a beautiful language," Swithin assured him. Swithin had learned it partly in a class, partly by studying a grammar book, but mainly by living in Italy with an Italian family. He was always looking for chances to practice it. "There are two ways to produce music vocally," he told this Rocco. "You can sing or you can speak Italian."

"Is that a saying?" Rocco asked.

"No," said Swithin, "I just thought of it."

"I suppose it's true," Rocco said. "I used to like to hear my cousins talk even when I couldn't understand what they were saying. It is musical." He added as an afterthought: "And I'm a musician!" He said it as though it was something that had just occurred to him. His tone of voice caused Swithin to look at him quizzically, but Rocco changed the subject again.

"My grandparents – both sets of grandparents – came from Italy to Wales to begin with..."

"Wales?" said Swithin.

"Cardiff, but later they moved to Brighton and then London. They made ice cream for a living, and it was very good ice cream, too. It was—is—a big tradition in our family. My dad ran Ritornelli's Fine Ice Cream – maybe you've heard of it? His pistacchio ice cream was famous."

Swithin felt a small pang of disappointment that Rocco pronounced pistacchio with a soft English sh sound and not the hard Italian c.

"It was more concentrated than the cheaper ice creams," Rocco said. "As in anything, if you cut corners it shows. Sooner or later it shows. Dad used to say that. You can't cut corners. Now my brother Luca runs the business."

"So the older brother inherited the business?" Swithin asked, because he knew about Italian habits of primogeniture and family businesses because of the family he had lived with in Rome.

"No, I'm the eldest son," said Rocco. "They wanted me to... My mother was so... My mother tried ... Mama really wanted me to make ice cream all my life!"

Rocco seemed a bit disturbed, as though there had been family rows about it. Swithin didn't enquire further, in case it was a touchy subject. But he needn't have worried. Rocco hardly missed a beat. "My dear Mama! She wouldn't take no for an answer! The arguments!" Rocco rolled his eyes. "Just because my father had this ice cream company and made excellent pistacchio ice cream and did very well as a result, just because he had made a great success of it, I was supposed to devote my life to it! I ask you!"

"So what did you really want to do instead?"

"Oh, it was always music. I played the piano and clarinet, but I really wanted to compose. I used to take some tune and play around with variations on it. I had a kind of knack for it. I would arrange things in different keys. Mama supported me up to a point, until she found out how serious I was. I had a good teacher. My teacher let me follow my inclinations. She saw I wanted a lot of theory so she gave me that. Most young students run a mile from it! I couldn't get enough!" Rocco chuckled. "Finally my mother saw how keen I was."

"She finally gave in?" Swithin asked.

"It wasn't easy," Rocco said. "I was never in any doubt, myself. But I didn't want to hurt her. I knew from early on that my future was not in ice cream. I knew it would have to be in music. But getting Mama to come round... My brother helped. Luca was the businessman. He liked overseeing things, keeping records, dealing with the bank – all that stuff."

"So it wasn't an insurmountable problem, then?" Swithin asked.

"Well, I didn't think so, myself, but Mama was so single-minded about me taking over the business. I don't know what she thought Luca would do. That wasn't the point. Luca wasn't the eldest. God, she was traditional! She was born in Italy, actually. I think that had an effect on her. My dad was born here – in Cardiff, I mean. He was a little more flexible, but when he died Mama started putting her own plan into effect, or trying to. Maybe it was her way of handling her grief. He died young. She wanted to run things the way she thought he would have done. Luca's running the business better than I ever could have run it anyway."

"So now you're a composer?" Swithin asked, even though Rocco Ritornelli wasn't really from Italy.

"Yes, I think I can finally say so. In fact, I'm having a small concert in the Purcell Room tomorrow night! I should have a leaflet about it here somewhere." Rocco rummaged in a soft-sided briefcase and then rummaged again but apparently couldn't find it.

"Tell me about it," Swithin said. Swithin likes classical music and used to go to concerts all the time when he was still in London. Cadogan Hall, Wigmore Hall, St. Johns Smith Square, all those places.

Rocco paused before going on. "My mother, as I told you, wanted me to continue in the family ice cream business."

Swithin nodded, as though to say, "Of course, of course."

"She insisted that I learned the business thoroughly. This was long before she finally relented and let me live my own life."

Swithin wondered why he was backtracking and going over this old family squabble again.

"She made me go out in the ice cream vans – on the rounds through the streets —and sell ice cream on a stick and all that. We had a cheaper line of ice cream sticks and cornettos and a type of soft ice cream. It was all right when I was 14 or 15– anything's a novelty then–but later it got to be a bit demeaning. Demeaning if you think you're the next

Stravinsky. So I changed all the tunes our vans played."

Swithin thought of the ice cream van that used to come round our street playing "Popeye the Sailor Man". "So what did you change them to?" he asked.

"Well," said Rocco. "Palestrina. Some Monteverdi. I arranged a Bach toccata for ice-cream van, and it wasn't easy. You know, the register on an ice cream van is very limited. My mother was a little horrified when she first heard it. 'But Rocco,' she said, 'that isn't what people expect. You have to give them what they expect.' But that's not what Dad did when he introduced our pistacchio. She didn't have an answer for that. That gave her pause. Finally the Monteverdi grew on her a bit. There's a certain skill in arranging for ice-cream van – getting it all in when you have a limited range to work with. It's quite a challenge. In that Monteverdi piece, for example, there were descant parts that I had to transpose down, then something else was too low for the range, and I had to..."

"So what's the concert at the Purcell Room?" Swithin asked.

"It's a selection of works for unaccompanied ice-cream van," Rocco answered.

"Are those original compositions or arrangements?" Swithin asked. Swithin is equal to anything.

"Well," said Rocco, "a bit of both, actually. I've tried some themes and variations. And I have an early fugue based on Beethoven's "Ode to Joy". I

45

convinced Mama that it was very suitable for an ice-cream van. It got people in the mood. I'm playing that tomorrow night. I wish I had a leaflet here." He patted his briefcase in a half-hearted way. "I'm doing some Palestrina of course, and tomorrow night is also the world premiere of a new composition dedicated to my father. It's called 'Pistacchio and Stracciatelli'. I think he would have liked it. I just wish he was here to hear it. He would have liked the tribute. Mama's coming, and my brother Luca. They've got the best seats in the Purcell Room. I saw to that."

"So the ice-cream van is going to be on the stage at the Purcell Room? It must have been a job getting it there," said Swithin, who has quite a practical streak.

"Oh yes! It was a first, actually. We couldn't get it up in the lift from the Artists' Entrance for the rehearsal. In the end I had to drive it through the foyer. That van has the best turning circle of any musical instrument you ever saw! It's going to look fantastic on the night! Tomorrow night! I'll drive it out on to the stage, take a bow, do a brief introduction, and then go straight into the Palestrina. That's partly because it's a sentimental favourite of mine and partly because Mama approves of Italian composers. She's finally agreed that it's in keeping."

"You drove it right through the foyer?" Swithin asked. "But there are steps..."

"We had ramps. I wondered if they were sturdy enough, but they worked a treat. They were stronger than they looked. We had to clear it with the management and three unions, but in the end it was fine."

"Do you have future plans, other concerts?" Swithin asked.

"I'm hoping for a slot at the Wigmore Hall," Rocco Ritornelli confided. That's always been my dream. I'm working on that. My agent is working on it. Now I've got an agent! My agent is going to see about the Wigmore Hall."

"Well," said Swithin, "it sounds as though you're really on your way."

"Yes," replied Rocco happily, "I think I am. It's been a struggle, but I think I'm getting there. I think Mama is proud of me, although she doesn't like to show it."

"I expect she is proud of you," said Swithin. "Maybe you'll see it tomorrow night."

Rocco had finished his latte by now and was picking up his briefcase.

"Good luck," Swithin said.

"I've found them!" exclaimed Rocco. "In the side pocket! Here's a leaflet. Here's two. Take them both. Give one to a friend. Maybe you can come?"

"Thank you," said Swithin. "I'll look at my diary. Good luck."

"Thank you," said the composer, and he walked toward the door humming something that Swithin couldn't quite put his finger on.

BOSCO

Students are usually well into their first year before they even find The Bohemian Pirate. It's fairly quiet — as you might expect — and the regular customers know each other. Swithin wrote some of his best stuff at those tables. Or rather, his table, because he always sat in the same place. Swithin used to say that people who want to talk go into a café, some little bar or restaurant, and they look around for somebody to tell their life story to. If somebody is sitting there reading a book or checking over a typescript or something like that, they think Ah! There is someone who wants to hear me talk! I don't know why, but it's true. I would have doubted it before Swithin told me about some of the people he met there.

Swithin is so good-hearted that he never discouraged them very much. I think he tried sometimes, but before long he was nodding sympathetically and asking them questions. So of course then they never went away.

One day he was sitting there with a cappuccino and a clipboard and a red pen, deep in thought, in another world of carefully ordered sentences. He was laying out a logical argument the way you put planks across mud to walk on.

There was another customer, a man called Bosco, who used to go there regularly, too, and now he came over and sat down heavily at Swithin's table. The table was really too small for two people to pretend that the other wasn't there. Swithin looked up from his clipboard and nodded at this Bosco.

Bosco had a folded newspaper with him, but he didn't open it out to read. He just sat there looking at his watch. "This is the ninth, isn't it?" he said to Swithin.

Swithin looked up again and said, "The ninth? Yes, the ninth. Today's the ninth."

Bosco looked at his watch again, because it was one of those watches that gave the date as well as the time.

"Today's the ninth of July," Bosco said with a sigh. He opened the paper and looked at the headlines on the front page for a moment. The paper was taking up more than his half of the table, and Swithin moved his clipboard closer to his coffee cup.

"Have you ever used a pendulum?" Bosco asked.

"A pendulum? You mean like on a clock?" Swithin asked.

"Not exactly. Just a pendulum by itself. Just a weight at the end of a string."

"What's that for?" asked Swithin. "If it's not part of a clock?"

"It tells the future," Bosco said.

"Oh yes?" Swithin said, glancing down at his clipboard. "How does it do that?" Swithin knew it was a mistake to start asking questions, because he would only get answers.

"You take a weight — I had a wooden thing like a light pull, a turned beech-wood object that tapers toward the end, the bottom end."

"Yes?" Swithin said, tapping his red pen on the clipboard. "That's the pendulum?"

"Yes," said Bosco. "You hold the string with this weight on the end, and then you ask it a question. It circles clockwise or anti-clockwise, according to whether the answer is yes or no."

"I see," said Swithin, although he wasn't really very interested. He glazed over when he heard about water dowsing or anything of that kind.

"I asked it questions."

"Who or what did you ask?" Swithin asked.

"I don't know. You just ask."

"But how do you know who or what..."

"Something answers. I don't know what it is," Bosco said hurriedly. "You get an answer."

"You should ask it about the lottery," Swithin remarked with a show of seriousness.

"It doesn't work that way. It just answers yes or no."

"You could ask, 'Should I buy British Gas shares now?'"

"Yes, you could ask that," Bosco said.

"So what did you ask?"

"I asked when I was going to die. I narrowed down the month and the day."

"And the year?" Swithin asked.

"I just did the month and day," Bosco replied.

"Why did you..."

"I just did. I don't know why. I was curious. I don't know. I was just thinking of questions, and I asked, I just asked it..."

"It's not actually verifiable, is it? I mean, you'll have to wait and see, and then so what?" Swithin said, because he is a very commonsensical person.

"But the problem is..." Bosco said. Swithin hadn't realized that they were talking about a problem. "The problem is that now I know..."

"Or think you know."

"OK, 'or think I know' the day I'm going to die. The day and the month, but not the year."

"You could ask it the year, and then you'd know exactly. Do you want to do that?"

"No! The month and the day is too much. I don't want to know the year, too."

"Well, it may be wrong anyway."

"I trust the pendulum."

"Well, so it may be right." Swithin was getting the feeling he had when people talked about being Pisces with Libra rising. "Has it ever been right about anything else?"

"Don't you ever wonder when you're going to die," Bosco asked.

"No," said Swithin. "Life keeps me too busy. I don't spend much time wondering about things that can't be verified."

"Knowledge can be a terrible thing," said Bosco. "If you know a thing, you can't 'unknow' it. You've got it. You have to carry it around with you."

"And you don't even know whether what you know is true. I wouldn't worry about it," Swithin said. "You could be hit by a bus..."

"Tomorrow." Bosco finished his sentence. "I know that. Life is uncertain. OK. But

The fact is that this particular day that the pendulum told me about comes round every year. For one day a year I have a terrible day. I wake up in the morning thinking, 'Is this it? Is this the day it will happen?' and all day it's there in my mind, and I can't concentrate on anything else. It's horrible."

"The next day must be a relief. When you survive and wake up the next morning, I mean," Swithin said.

"That's quite true," said Bosco. "The rest of the year, in fact, is fine, except that as this date in July approaches I begin to get nervous. The week before the date I start thinking, 'Maybe it will be this time next week. Maybe my funeral will be in another fortnight. Maybe, you know, before I finish the current jar of coffee I'll be in my coffin. I think of that when I'm going round Sainsbury's."

"I suppose," Swithin said, looking longingly at his clipboard, "you could use the pendulum again and find out the exact year, and then you might have a nice relaxed life for a while and not worry at all. Until, of course, that particular year approached. That could be sticky."

"I wouldn't dare do that!" said Bosco. "If I knew for certain the exact time—the day, month, and year—I would be like a man on an ice floe with Niagara Falls ahead. True enough, maybe it wouldn't be now, maybe it wouldn't even be next year or the year after that, but it would be sitting there and the time between it and the present would be narrowing all the time. I don't think I could bear it. No, it would be awful to know the whole truth."

"So, as it is, you know two-thirds of the truth, is that it? Would it have been better to know the year and not the month? Or the day but not the month? The worst thing would be to know the year and the month, because then you would be a nervous wreck for 30 days, or 31 in the case of seven of the months. But then, if it was a day in February, you would have only 28 days to be worried. Twenty-nine in a leap year, of course." Swithin was going off on one of his tangents. This proved that he wasn't being serious about the man's dilemma.

"I've thought of all that!" Bosco said. "I know what I know. There's nothing that can be done about it. I don't want to know the year."

"You are in the odd position of someone who wished to know what he now doesn't want to know, and who doesn't want to know the one remaining fact in this set. I use the word 'fact' loosely. You didn't foresee this problem?"

"I wasn't thinking about it at all. I was just thinking...I don't know what I was thinking. I was just asking it random questions. I was asking it obvious things, like 'Is my tie red, yes or no?' and 'Is my mother's name Elizabeth?' and 'Was the Battle of Trafalgar fought in October?' and then I thought I would ask it questions that I myself didn't know the answers to. I thought, 'Why not try to learn something instead of just playing games?' and so I asked it a question or two that occurred to me. I wanted to know something about myself, you know, something that would be useful."

"This does not actually sound very useful," Swithin murmured. "Perhaps you might have asked about something that would soon happen that you could check. Like, 'Will I be delayed on the Northern Line tomorrow?' Then, come the next day, you could see whether it had been right. And as the Northern Line is out of your control (or indeed, it sometimes seems, anybody's) you would not be able to influence the outcome of the thing. If this object of yours said yes or no, you would not be able to make it happen that way, even unconsciously. You could then be sure that this pendulum was telling the truth. Or not. On that occasion, anyway. On the other hand, there would be a 50/50 chance either way, so it still might not prove a great deal about the general veracity of the device. Nevertheless, it might give you some idea."

The man had been listening intently, but Swithin's remarks weren't much good to him now. The deed had been done. He knew what he knew and was terrified to learn more. Swithin couldn't decide whether he was a sort of Faust character or just gullible.

"I'm fed up with the pendulum. I destroyed it when I realized what it had done to me. It's ruined my life!"

Swithin looked at the man sitting on the other side of his table. He was dejected and fidgeted distractedly with his sugar packet until he tore it and the sugar fell out on the table. Then he nervously swept the sugar granules off on to the floor with a shaky hand. "Look," said Swithin. "The damage has been done. It's ruined your life. But you don't really know whether it's true or not, and you won't know until the last moment of your life. You are assuming that it is true, but you might just as logically assume that its information is false, since you don't know for sure. You can't ignore it. You could experiment with this gadget some more, and you might find that it doesn't know what it's talking about. If you do find out that it is right most of the time (which would surprise me), then you won't be any more unhappy than you already are. If you find that it is wrong much of the time, and you might suspect that it will be wrong about your big question you put to it, and then you might be less agitated when the fateful day rolls round."

Bosco looked up from fiddling with the empty sugar packet. "Yes. But I threw the damned thing away. I don't know whether I want to touch one again."

"Suit yourself," said Swithin. "I don't blame you. But I thought you might try this as a way of learning more. Or verifying the accuracy of the device."

"I can't be perfectly sure that it works," said Bosco as though no one had mentioned this idea before. "I could ask it some innocent questions about the weather or something like that. I could say, 'Will it rain here next Thursday?' It has to answer yes or no. It can't say, 'Chances of showers in the South'. It can't say, 'Scattered showers with sunny intervals'. It would have to come down on one side or the other. And the thing is" – he jabbed an index finger at Swithin – "it would be verifiable! I would know on the following Thursday, for example, whether it was right or wrong."

"I believe you would," Swithin murmured.

"But suppose I find out that the gadget is 100% correct on everything? Then there's no way out. Then it will be correct about this terrible date. Instead of only being afraid that I will die on that day, I will be certain of it! Could I bear that? What would I do then?"

"I should certainly ask it about the Lottery. You could frame the questions to require a yes or no answer. Then you could at least live in style until the date came round again."

Bosco smiled for the first time. "I could live in style," he mused.

"It would take your mind off things," Swithin said.

"I need string and a weight. A piece of string." Bosco brushed some more sugar off on to the floor and stood up. "I think I'll be off, then," he said. "Thanks for the suggestion."

"Don't mention it," Swithin murmured.

THE BEE-KEEPER

My brother Swithin is usually attracted to cheerful people, but when the middle-aged woman came into The Bohemian Pirate looking so sad he couldn't help wondering what the matter was. He tried not to stare. She ordered a cappuccino and looked around the café in a despairing sort of way. She must have seen Swithin looking in her direction and she slowly made her way to his table, even though there were other empty tables. Swithin resigned himself to having company. Maybe she would just sit there and look into her coffee cup and he could get on with his work. He was well along with his book then and putting his arguments together and assembling his material and so on.

The woman sat down and Swithin acknowledged her with a little nod but went on with his writing. She had a medium build and was wearing slightly dowdy clothes. Her shoes were practical and scuffed. Swithin thought she might be a bag lady if only she had some bags.

But when she spoke she sounded well educated. She had been looking to one side at the floor, then at the coffee on the table in front of her, and then absently in Swithin's direction. As he had just looked up again and their eyes met, she said, "Have you ever kept bees, by any chance?"

"No," said Swithin, "I never have. Do you keep bees?" Swithin could never resist getting into conversations with people, for all the talk about interruptions.

"I used to keep bees," she said, and Swithin was afraid that she was going to cry. "We live in Surrey. It's good country for bees. We have trees and...chestnuts with those wonderful candles...and the farmers roundabout grow broad beans." When she spoke of the "wonderful candles" her tone of voice sounded as though she were saying "horrible candles". Her voice seemed full of regret and despair.

"Well," said Swithin, a bit nonplussed. "They say it's a fine hobby. I once knew a bee-keeper in Italy, and..."

"Oh, it is a fine hobby, as you say!" she exclaimed. "But it's not really a hobby, young man, it's a way of life! A bee-keeper is...Keeping bees is very special. It's...it's...this may sound strange to you, but it's a privilege. Keeping bees is a privilege!"

Swithin was afraid he had a depressed fanatic on his hands.

"Of course," she went on, "not everyone wants to keep bees. Of course. People have different tastes, different predilections. But, bees... Well, of course you don't get to know them, it's not like having a dog or cat, it's not quite like having pets, but at the same time you do have a feeling for them collectively. You have a few hives and you feel protective about them, the way you would look after a regular four-footed pet. You check up on them, you keep them warm in the winter."

"Do you, or I mean did you, have many hives?" Swithin asked.

"We had six hives," she said morosely.

"Was there..." Swithin knew he was on dangerous territory, "a virus? Or a parasite of some sort?" He spoke softly as though he were enquiring after her own health.

"Oh no," she said. "They were healthy bees! They were fine, healthy bees! You know, they don't really sting. They don't sting as much as they're made out to. You can put your hands right down among them and feel their little furry bodies, and they don't usually sting. In my whole life I've been stung only three or four times. I think they know you're looking out for them, taking care of them."

This was news to Swithin. When he was little he was terrified of bees and wasps. He was stung once when he was a tot and I think it affected him for life.

"You're young," she said. "You could keep bees. Even if you live in town you could keep them. There are lots of people who live in cities and keep bees. You'd be surprised. There's an apiary supply place not far from here. I've just come from there. I wanted to talk to someone about bees, and we've got some used equipment I thought they might sell for us. You might enjoy having some bees!"

The very idea horrified Swithin. "I'm sure it is a great satisfaction to keep bees," he said. "But I don't think I have the necessary...I don't have the time to...and then unfortunately I live in a flat. I don't have anywhere to put a hive."

"You would need some space, of course, although not very much. They don't take up very much room, considering the pleasure they give, to say nothing of the honey." She smiled at Swithin. "We had so much honey. We gave it away as presents and we sold it at fairs and fetes. We had some labels made up. There would be just enough profit to cover our expenses. We didn't do it for the money."

She absent-mindedly picked up her coffee cup and tested the temperature. She put it down again and picked up a sugar packet. She carefully tore the top edge off and dribbled the sugar into her coffee, where it settled on top of the froth and then sank.

"So you don't keep bees anymore?" Swithin asked.

"No. No more bees. We've stopped keeping bees."

Now she stirred her coffee, making little figure-8s in the cappuccino froth. She took a spoonful of chocolate-sprinkled frothy milk and put it in her mouth. In a moment she said, "We lost all our bees. They were killed. All six hives."

"Killed?" said Swithin. "What killed them?"

"They were stepped on," the woman said.

"Somebody stepped on all six hives of your bees?" Swithin asked. He found that he didn't feel sorry for the bees because he was sure that they would have stung him if they had ever got half a chance, but he couldn't imagine how anyone could step on a hive of bees. Now he was afraid he had a crazy depressed fanatic on his hands, although she had seemed like a pleasant enough woman in the beginning.

"They missed a few," she said bitterly. "But the survivors couldn't sustain a whole hive by themselves. Poor little things. Poor little lost bees!"

Swithin felt a little perplexed. The woman seemed sad and angry about these bees, but Swithin still felt that they were only one step up from mosquitoes and he didn't even like honey very much. Furthermore, her story was beginning to sound preposterous.

"We live down in Little Stokeham. You get there from Waterloo," she said. "Our station is quite pretty with original valencing and hanging baskets."

Swithin was startled by this sudden change of subject. He really wondered if the woman was quite sane. First it was bees and now she was off on this village and the local amenities! Whatever next?

"One day down at the station there was a barrel of beer that got broken open and the beer ran all over the down platform. There were big puddles of it. Our bees were attracted to it. Beer has quite a high sugar content, you know. They...well, they got drunk! I suppose it doesn't take very much alcohol to make a bee drunk, and they were unable to fly. They were crawling about on the platform just when people were coming down from London in the evening, and they stepped on them! I think some of them couldn't help it, because the bees were everywhere, but others stamped on them on purpose. I find that simply sickening, to stamp on a little honey bee! Don't you think? Oh, it really makes me sick!"

"And that's how all of your hives were destroyed?" Swithin asked.

"Yes. There were thousands of bees on that platform, and by the time the stationmaster called us, the damage had been done and they were all, or most of them, dead. All our little bees!"

"That certainly is a sad story," Swithin said, "but can't you get some more bees? I know it wouldn't be the same, but..."

"No, we're not going to replace them. Of course we could replace them. It's not as though we had given them all names! One individual bee is much like another. It's just that we don't want to start over. It takes a certain amount of strength and energy, you know, and we're neither of us getting any younger. Clifford hasn't been well this last year. And then..." her voice trailed off.

"But perhaps just one hive?" Swithin said.

"Not even one. We just haven't the heart to go through it all again. After what happened. Perhaps you find it ridiculous. It certainly has its ridiculous side. Our grandson thought it was quite hilarious. But you know, we would always wonder if some other strange accident might befall them sometime."

"Surely," said Swithin, "nothing so bizarre would happen a second time."

"Maybe not. But the hive would remind us of what had happened to the others and how people had been so gratuitously cruel to our bees. I used to have nightmares about it," she confided.

"You mean nightmares about your bees being stepped on?"

"Yes. Sometimes I was a bee crawling on the platform and big feet were stamping all around me. Sometimes I would come to the station and find all the commuters trampling the bees in a sort of mad frenzy. I would always wake in a panic and then I couldn't get back to sleep. It didn't seem to bother Clifford so much. He would say, 'Well, what's done is done.' He would try to cheer me up. He would say, 'Oh well, that was first-rate beer. They died happy.' Somehow it just made me sadder about what had happened."

Swithin had begun to feel sorry for her. She was so obviously miserable about her bees. "Well," he said – because he was always trying to solve people's problems for them – "is there some other aspect of beekeeping with which you could occupy yourself? For example, could you teach beginners how to look after bees? Or perhaps there is some organisation for bee fanciers? You could..."

"I'm already the secretary of the North Surrey Beekeepers' Association. I've always been involved with all aspects of beekeeping. Poor little things. They couldn't help it. They didn't know what they were doing. They got into that beer, and the next thing they knew...they must have been dizzy. They couldn't fly and they had lost their sense of direction. My poor little bees! And by the time we got there it was too late. Oh, I can't think about it anymore!"

But she seemed to be thinking about it all the time. Swithin felt he was present at a bereavement and anything he might say would sound inadequate or mawkish. He almost shivered at the thought of the horrible little insects, furry and cuddly though they might be to some. Little stinging creatures. You could die of a bee sting! You could have an allergic reaction and die! Little tiny killers is what they were!

"Young man," the woman said kindly, "I see my story has affected you deeply. I'm sorry to have made you sad, too. I didn't mean to burden you with my sorrow. I've had a considerable shock, but I am learning to live with it. Your life moves on, you know. Perhaps it was time for me to stop keeping bees anyway. I would have gone on until I dropped. Now I must do something else. I will just spend more time on my patchwork quilts. We all have to make these adjustments. You may be too young to know about that yet."

Maybe Swithin took to heart what she said about life moving on and making adjustments.

"I'm very sorry to hear about the sad demise of your bees," he said sincerely.

THE SWIMMING INSTRUCTOR

My brother Swithin used to say that the thing about Dutch women was that they all looked like swimming instructors. I don't know where Swithin had met so many Dutch women that he could make such sweeping generalisations about them. I've been to Holland a few times, and I've seen lots of Dutch women who did not look particularly like swimming teachers. They could have been anything, but Swithin always had this odd stereotype about them. He had a weakness for them, but in the end he married an American.

One day one of these "swimming instructors" came into The Bohemian Pirate when he was there. For once it was crowded enough that there really wasn't another unoccupied table and she asked Swithin if the place was taken. He said no, it wasn't, not at all, please sit down. She got engrossed in writing postcards and didn't pay much more attention to him, but he had heard her accent and surmised correctly that she was from Holland. He saw that she was writing "The Netherlands" at the bottom of the addresses on her postcards. She was slender and blonde with rather short hair that would dry quickly. She was bending over her cards and he couldn't see the colour of her eyes, but they must be blue – as blue as the sea, as blue as a swimming pool.

It was one of those rare times when Swithin wanted to start a conversation with someone sitting at his table. He gazed at the blonde woman bent over her postcards. "You're writing postcards to your friends," he said. "Postcards of London," he said, as though she might be sitting in London sending cards depicting some other place.

"Yes," she said without looking up. Swithin was about to try another gambit when she finished her card and said, "As a matter of fact, I was writing to a boy I've been coaching in English. His name is Jeroen. He's the son of some friends of mine in the little town where I live and he needs a lot of help. So I am helping him with his English. If he doesn't pass his English test he will have to repeat the whole year. So his mother asked me if I would give him extra lessons two times a week and I said yes."

"Your English is very good," Swithin said.

"Thank you," said the blonde Dutchwoman.

"Do you teach English? In a school, I mean?" Swithin asked.

"I used to, before my children came along," she said. "After that I have just taught when the usual teacher is sick. And a little individual tutoring, like this." She looked right at him with her blue eyes.

"Let me introduce myself," said Swithin, who had never willingly introduced himself to a stranger in the Bohemian Pirate before. "My name is Swithin."

"And I'm Ria," she said. "Swidden," she repeated. "That's an unusual name."

"Yes," Swithin said, charmed by her mispronunciation. "It's the name of an old English saint. My parents thought it should be reintroduced."

"Quite original people, your parents."

"So you're teaching this boy English? Is he applying himself to his lessons? Is he going to pass this exam?"

"I think he's trying, but he is a little bit lazy. He is probably intelligent enough, but he has many distractions and would prefer to play computer games. He is like many boys of his age. And like many energetic boys he has been in trouble."

"Trouble?" Swithin said, "What did he do?"

"He was a very foolish boy. Jeroen and three other boys from our town vandalised a holiday home. Our town is in a tourist area near the sea and there are many small houses where visitors come in the summer and for weekends, mostly from Germany. This house was very nice. It had a lot of expensive things in it, like a television and a music centre and a computer – that kind of thing. Jeroen and his friends broke into the house one Saturday night and just destroyed all those expensive things!"

"The television, the computer..." Swithin murmured.

"And the music centre with four separate speakers and a number of tapes and CDs," Ria added. "His parents, who are very good people by the way, asked him why he did it, and he could never explain why. He didn't say, 'We thought it was fun' or 'We thought it was daring and exciting' or even 'We didn't like the owner'. In fact they didn't know the owner. He was a very nice dentist from Dusseldorf, as it happened. A kind and gentle man who couldn't understand why those Dutch boys had ruined his house. He was very sad and upset. I felt very sorry for him."

"Did the boy regret what he'd done?" Swithin asked.

"Yes, very much," Ria said. "He was full of remorse. His parents made him go and apologise to the dentist and his wife. They came that weekend and found their house ruined. All this destroyed equipment was lying all over the floor. The dentist went to the police, who quickly found Jeroen and his friends. We were sorry it happened to a foreigner, you know, and especially a German, because we like to have good relations with them now. Some people still resent them because of the War, but that's all in the past. We all felt embarrassed, terribly embarrassed."

Swithin gazed at the tender-hearted blonde Dutchwoman who had felt embarrassed because stupid teenagers had vandalised a German's house. He was helplessly charmed by her tender-heartedness and her embarrassment and her blondeness. "Of course you felt embarrassed," he said.

"Jeroen's parents were very upset about it. They took flowers to the German couple and invited them to dinner as a way of apologising for it. They made Jeroen sit at the table and talk to these people whose house he helped to destroy. I think he felt horrible about it. Well, it would have been

68

very awkward for him! He was such a foolish boy! And that was his punishment. I think he learned the lesson. There was the official punishment too."

"Did he tell you about this dinner? Is that how you know he learned his lesson?"

"He was too embarrassed to say much about it. He's at that age when everything is very painful and puzzling. But even without his telling me, we live in a small town and everyone, from the mayor to the florist, already knew everything. For a week or two after the event you would go into, for example, the bakery and everyone would be talking about it. You would hear someone say, 'The damage was 25,000 guilders, you know,' and someone else would say, 'I heard it was a wide-screen television and cost 3,000 guilders' and so on. It's a very small town. It has its disadvantages sometimes. Jeroen can't go anywhere without people looking at him and thinking, 'Just think, that boy did 30,000 guilders' worth of damage'— because the amount keeps increasing as people tell the story! And of course Jeroen knows it. He knows what the people in the town think about him. He is surprised that no one trusts him anymore! He didn't realise that now no one would leave him in a room with anything valuable!"

"It's good of you to help him," Swithin said.

"Well, you have to," she said. "What would happen if you didn't? Somebody has to put him back on the right track. He has to finish school. If he does reasonably well, he will have too much self-respect to be a burglar and a vandal. That's the theory anyway." She smiled at Swithin and he thought that Jeroen had no excuse not to reform his life.

"This young man is very lucky to have someone like you to help him," Swithin said daringly.

"Thank you," she said, smiling again. "You do what you can, and I'm very fond of his parents. Jeroen had an older sister who was in my class, I mean a class I taught. She was quite clever, and I suspect Jeroen is too, if he would just try a little bit."

"What do you teach him?" Swithin asked, not wanting her to go back to her postcards. "How do you help him?"

"I try not to be too judgemental. He knows that I disapprove of what he did, and so I don't have to keep bringing it up. In Dutch we have a saying, 'to drag the cow out of the ditch' – de kou uit het sloot halen – and that means to keep bringing up an unpleasant subject, so I don't keep 'dragging the cow out of the ditch', so to say. I try to concentrate on the positive aspects – the fact that he is sorry about what he did and wants to learn. He comes to my house every Tuesday and Thursday afternoon for an hour and we work on his school lessons with some extra work on the problem areas. Prepositions, verb tenses, all sorts of things. We sit in the living room and drink tea. I try to make it welcoming and cosy for him, what we call gezellig. It is a pity that there is no equivalent in English for that word, it is so useful. Anyway, I think he appreciates it."

"He should appreciate your efforts," Swithin said.

"Do you know why I have some hope for him? Why I think he might be going back on the right track?"

"No. Why do you think so?" Swithin really wanted to know.

"I told you we sit in my living room. I always sit in a certain chair. It is a large chair covered with dark leather. Jeroen sits in a smaller wooden chair which is normally about two metres away, so he has to bring it closer to my chair so that we can look at his books together."

"Oh yes?" Swithin said politely, not quite seeing the point, but thinking it would be very nice to sit close to her.

"After we finish he puts his chair back exactly where it was before. I have seen him very carefully placing it back so that the four legs of that chair are on the same little marks in the rug. You see, he doesn't want to make new marks on my rug! It's his way of trying to make amends. He's not really a bad boy."

"But this German dentist is not getting much benefit from the boy's amends. It's a bit late for this exaggerated care in putting your chair back in its place."

"Fortunately the insurance covered it, but the magistrate is making Jeroen and his friends pay back a proportion of the value of all this equipment and furniture. Then they have to do some community service, too. He is gradually learning to be responsible for his actions. And perhaps we are also learning to be a little bit responsible for him." She smiled at Swithin again with her captivating smile. "If we let things follow their own course they would probably turn out badly. It's all in seeing what it is possible to do."

Swithin thought about what it might be possible to do. "Would you like another cup of coffee?" he said.

CAFÉ TABLES

My brother Swithin used to say that Ronan wasn't really meant for the theatre. Swithin couldn't imagine him on the stage in any role, except possibly that of a proprietor of a coffee shop. Ronan wanted to call it a coffeehouse because of the echo of the atmospheric old London coffeehouses. The Bohemian Pirate never resembled an 18th century coffeehouse, either in Swithin's time or later when I knew the place. Ronan and his partners had just bought the place as a business for when they weren't appearing in a stage play, which was most of the time. The name of The Bohemian Pirate even had some theatrical connection, evidently. It was some kind of Shakespearean reference. Ronan seemed to have a flair for the business. The others, Keith and Fleur, were also very good coffee makers and café proprietors, but it was always a secondary profession with them. Definitely a day job. They were always on the look-out for an audition. Ronan became more and more on the look-out for an improved coffee machine or smarter crockery.

Ronan took a break one spring before the summer season, if you could say that The Bohemian Pirate had any kind of season. There seemed to be a small but steady flow of customers

– people who somehow managed to find the place in its courtyard off a side street. In London people and traffic are both like water – they eventually seep into any place where there's an empty space. So Ronan went to Paris with some friends for a few days, and when he came back he saw the Bohemian Pirate with new eyes.

"We should wear proper aprons," he said to the others.

"Aprons?" Fleur said. "For the washing up?"

"No, aprons all the time. Like in France. The waiters all wear long white wrap-around aprons. It makes them look very professional."

"It makes them look like French waiters," Keith said. "I'd feel pretentious, myself, wearing an apron down to my ankles."

So Ronan had suggested something French and pretentious and the others weren't keen, but he kept thinking about the Parisian cafés he had visited.

"Research," he said. "I was doing research, you know. I wasn't just hanging out in cafés like a total tourist. No, I was observing. I was watching how things were done, and I learned a lot. All kinds of things."

"What did you learn?" Swithin asked.

"Oh, about serving drinks on trays..."

"But," Fleur said, "we don't serve at the tables. People get their stuff at the counter and then go to a table."

"Still, it was all useful," Ronan said. "It's about style. The way to do things. The way to move around the place. The little flourishes. We could try some flourishes. Add a little pizzazz to things."

"Pizzazz he wants!" Fleur said, throwing up her hands like Bette Midler.

"For example, here's one thing. We could have a few tables and chairs out on the pavement. That's what people like in hot weather. And a ceiling fan. We could put a ceiling fan in. That adds character to a place."

"A job for Beaufort," said Keith. "Beaufort could do it in no time."

"Who's Beaufort?" Swithin asked.

"He's our handyman," Keith said.

"Handyman!" Fleur said. "He's a lot more than a handyman! He can fix anything! He's an electrician and plasterer and bricklayer! He's..."

"He's a genius," Ronan said. "He'd be the one to do it, all right."

In the meantime Ronan got four small round zinc-topped tables and matching chairs and put them out in front of The Bohemian Pirate, two on each side of the door. They had been out there for three days when The Bohemian Pirate was more or less raided by the police. Two bobbies came in and didn't look like they'd come for a cup of latte. They went up to Keith and asked if he was the manager. He said he was one of the joint managers. They said that he would need a license from the council to put semi-permanent objects used in the pursuit of his business on the highway in front of his premises.

"I'm sorry," said Keith. "We didn't know that was necessary."

"You'll have to take them back in until you get the license. Sorry," they said. "They usually come through within 30 days."

"Thirty days!" Ronan exclaimed. "But the sitting-out-on-the-pavement season will be half over by then! And this being England, the summer could be entirely over by then."

The policemen seemed sympathetic. They shrugged sympathetically. "You'll know for next year. You have to renew the license every year."

"How much is it?" Keith asked.

"Don't know. Fifty pounds. Maybe a hundred. Not all that much for a prosperous business like yours," said one of the policemen.

"Does everybody have to pay for a license? All those places in Leicester Square? All the pubs and cafés with tables out..."

"Well," said the policeman, "it depends on the council. That's Westminster, of course. They're raking it in from other sources. But maybe they charge, too. Don't know, really. I imagine it's so much a table. You need to see to it, all right?"

When the policemen had left, Ronan said, "I'll bet this doesn't happen in Paris."

"But," Fleur said, "Paris has to raise money, too. They have to keep the city running, have to clean it."

"Clean it!" said Keith. "Do they still have signs all over the place telling you not to spit on things? I went on a school trip once, and all I remember are the signs telling you not to spit on this and that— ne pas cracher sur whatever it was. And not to pee on things, either! We were fourteen. 'Don't pee on the famous building"! It gave a boost to our French, anyway, going around translating the signs telling you not to..."

"I don't think the French spit on things anymore," said Ronan, who had become a Francophile after three days in Paris cafés. "If they ever did."

"They must have done," Keith said, "or else they wouldn't have to tell them not to. You don't have to tell people not to do things they don't do anyway. You don't have to put up signs saying..."

"Look," Ronan said, "the point is that we have to apply for this bloody license from the Council. So how do we do that? Where's the Council office, anyway?"

Fleur knew and said she would make enquiries and get the forms. Ronan's enthusiasm for recreating a French café in that courtyard off a side street was dampened somewhat. Fleur and Ronan were the ones who generally did most of the paperwork, and in the next few days they began the process for getting consent to place amenities on the public highway in accordance with the Highway Act of 1980.

Keith, meanwhile, had been offered an audition at the New End Theatre in Hampstead.

"It's not the West End," he said, "but it is a good theatre and a performance is a performance. The critics notice the New End. It's not obscure. It's not upstairs over some pub in Bounds Green, you know."

"No," said Fleur. "You go for it. We can manage here. And maybe Swithin would help out."

They were standing within earshot of Swithin's table, and Fleur raised her voice slightly with her last sentence. Swithin didn't seem to hear. If Swithin was reading something, he probably really didn't hear. He wasn't the kind to pretend to be deaf when someone wanted his help.

"There's nothing wrong with Bounds Green," Ronan said.

"Swithin," Fleur said, "Keith has to go for an audition on Thursday. We want him to go, but we may need a little help now and then behind the counter, you know, filling in a bit while Keith is away. Do you think you could bear to lend a hand here and there?"

"Why not?" Swithin said, trying to seem enthusiastic. "Show me what to do."

They decided that he might be best employed on the cash register, so they took him behind the counter and showed him how it worked.

"You could collect the crockery and clean off the tables, too, if we're short-handed. I mean," Fleur said, "it may not get that busy, but if it does, we'd be glad to think that we could count on you. It'll only be for half a day or so."

"All right. I'll give it a go," Swithin said.

"Next Thursday," Fleur reminded him.

On Thursday Swithin was getting the hang of the work in the café and rather enjoying it, although he had left his books and clipboard at his usual table so that when things were slow he could go back to being a customer. One of the perks was free coffee for the day, and Swithin was trying out the mocha when there was a shout from the little staff/utility room. Water was dripping down the wall from upstairs and making an expanding puddle on the floor.

"Fleur!" Ronan shouted. "Get Beaufort! I'm going upstairs to see what's going on! Swithin, look after things!"

Swithin took up his position behind the counter, hoping that if anyone came in they would want filter coffee or mocha, since those were his specialties so far.

"Where's his phone number?" Fleur shouted to Ronan. "What's his last name?"

"Beaufort's not his last name?" Swithin asked.

"It's in the book," Ronan called back on his way to the outside door. "The book by the phone. Under S for Simmons. Ask him if he can come asap! Tell him it's an emergency!" Ronan ran out to the entrance door for the upstairs flat and rang the bell. Swithin could hear him yelling into the intercom at the door. The upstairs neighbours of The Bohemian Pirate were a Greek family who sometimes came in and said the coffee was really quite good, considering.

Someone seemed to be at home and in a moment they could hear Ronan's footsteps pounding up the stairs to the Tsolikides' flat. Ronan and Mrs. Tsolikides seemed to be doing a lively peasant dance overhead, but in fact they were looking for the stopcock to get the water turned off. The water was still pouring down the wall of the utility room and Fleur was putting buckets and rags on the floor to catch it and keep it from running out into the café. At the same time she was looking under S in the little phone book that was kept under the telephone.

Swithin, standing authoritatively behind the cash register, could hear part of her conversation with Beaufort Simmons. Fleur had called him on his mobile and got straight through to him.

"Beaufort? Oh, thank God! This is Fleur at The Bohemian Pirate. We've got a ghastly emergency here! Water is simply gushing down the wall from upstairs! I know you're terribly busy, but could you possibly come? Are you anywhere near here at the moment? Oh, that's not too far! We'd be eternally grateful if...Could you really? It's terrible. Ronan's gone upstairs to try to get it stopped, but...Right. Oh, right. So we'll see you soon? Honestly, we'd be so....Thanks so much, Beaufort! Thanks a lot!"

Fleur came out to Swithin at the cash register. "He's coming! I hope the insurance covers this. It ought to, oughtn't it? Anyway, he could pretty much drop everything and come! Stroke of luck, really."

When Beaufort Simmons arrived he turned out to be a West Indian with dreadlocks. "Hi," he said to Swithin. "Where's Fleur? Man, she call me all in a panic about this water dripping down. Well, you put it in a tank high up, and it got nowhere else to drip but down!" He laughed as though there were no particular emergency.

Ronan had come back downstairs by then, having been unable to find the Tsolikides' stopcock. "Beaufort," he said, "come upstairs with me! I've found where it's coming from."

"Right!" said Beaufort. "Show me where that water coming from. We'll get it fix, no problem." He picked up his bag of tools and strolled after Ronan.

Fleur had gone back to manning the coffee machine. "And there won't be a problem, either, now that he's here! He's saved our bacon a couple of times. He's really an electrician, but he can turn his hand at anything. He rewired this place, you know, when we first took it over."

After Beaufort had diagnosed the problem, turned off the stopcock, and repaired the leak, he came back down to The Bohemian Pirate. "You got water damage down here?" he asked them.

"Have a look," said Fleur, "It didn't do the wall any good. Will it dry out all right?" She was taking him to the back room.

"What it didn't do no good to was the ceiling," Beaufort Simmons was saying, and Swithin could hear the two of them discussing the wet patch overhead. He couldn't always make out what Beaufort was saying because until you got used to his rich accent you would miss a few words or phrases.

While Swithin was behind the counter the two policemen came in again to see the license for the pavement tables, and Ronan was able to show them the new license, which had set them back £75 but was well worth it because it had already paid for itself.

"You see?" said one of the policemen, "That wasn't so hard, was it? Now it's good for twelve months. You can also get one of those heaters like a lamppost and use it all year round. Then again, I don't know if there's room out there. It's a public right-of-way, you know, much as the place looks like a cul-de-sac. There's barely room for the tables. If the pavement was any narrower, it'd be an obstruction. But you're OK."

He turned to the second policeman and said, "We could take a break. How about a cup of their coffee? You don't have to have cappuccino."

"We could do you a nice mocha," Swithin said.

"Whatever," said the second policeman. "Put some sugar in it."

"The sugar's at the end of the counter," Swithin replied. "Help yourself."

Beaufort Simmons emerged from the utility room to see the two policemen sitting at a table poking at their frothy cups with little spoons. He stopped in his tracks and Swithin saw that he seemed more alarmed now than he had been at the prospect of a water feature in the back room. "Man, what those cops doing there?" he asked Ronan with his hand over his mouth. "Those guys not looking for me, are they?"

"No, they just dropped in to check our license for the tables and chairs out on the pavement. They're just having a break now. Would you like some coffee, too? It's on the house."

Beaufort really looked as though he needed to sit down. Swithin wondered what kind of run-in he had had with the police. He hadn't thought of this wizard plumber and electrician and so on having a problem with the men in blue. Maybe he had been stopped and searched unnecessarily, as apparently often happened to non-white people in London.

That would make you wary of the constabulary. Beaufort Simmons was in his early thirties and seemed to be a competent, hard-working chap. Did the cops think he had a sideline in crime?

"Yeah," said Beaufort, "OK, but me got to get back to work. We doing a job at King Edward and I been away too long already."

"You have to take the odd break," Fleur said. "Anyway, think of it as customer relations. It would be a pleasure to serve you a cup of our best coffee! What'll you have? How about the Colombian dark roast? How about a latte? Or you could have an espresso if you prefer. Or a double espresso."

"You got decaffeinated coffee?" Beaufort asked. "I don't need no caffeine. It not so good for you, yeah? That stuff keep me awake at night. What I really like is Darjeeling tea, kinda weak, no milk. You got fruit juice?"

"We've got some very nice orange juice, grapefruit juice, and some lovely new mango and passion fruit juice. Does any of that appeal?" Fleur was trying hard to make a sale, and it wasn't even a sale.

Beaufort, with his liking for weak tea and fruit juice, was sounding less and less like a drug dealer to Swithin. Still, for some reason the police made him nervous.

There was hardly anyone else in The Bohemian Pirate just then. When the police had finished and gone on their way, Fleur nodded and smiled at Swithin to show that he could leave his post at the cash register if he wanted to. Swithin made a free latte for himself as Fleur was getting the fruit juice out of the cooler and pouring it for Beaufort.

Swithin sat down at his accustomed table and indicated the other chair at his table. "Have a seat," he said to Beaufort.

"Thanks, man," he said. "I can stay a couple minutes, but I got guys waiting for me."

"When they said they were going to call Beaufort, I thought that was your last name."

"No, man, that my Christian name! My mama was carrying me, see, and they was a hurricane coming. They was all talking about this and that on the Beaufort Scale, this storm was eleven, then it was twelve on this Beaufort Scale, yeah? The more they talk about it, the more my mama thought, 'Say, that a nice name for my baby! "Beaufort", that got a bit of class!' So that what happen! She told my daddy that they was no two ways about it, that baby was going to be Beaufort. My daddy was busy with his work and he already had six kids, so he let her choose. "Beaufort" was OK with him. They always people want to shorten it to 'Beau', but I tell them 'No,' I say, 'My name's Beaufort!'" Beaufort laughed and slapped the table top lightly.

"Good for you," Swithin said. "Don't let people try to shorten your name for you." Nobody had ever got very far trying to shorten Swithin's name, but he knew what it was like to go through life with an unusual name.

Beaufort Simmons finished his orange juice and stood up. "I got to get back to my job. Got to keep to the schedule." Then he turned to Fleur. "Look, me come back and check that plaster, yeah? Don't want that roof falling in on you!" He picked up his satchel of tools and went back to King Edward College, his composure restored by the orange juice.

THE WOMAN ON THE BUS

"Do you think I could have a pot of Earl Grey tea, please?" the woman asked Fleur. She had just come in looking a bit flustered and footsore, and she was well past the first flush of youth, or even the second or third one.

"Of course," Fleur answered. "Take a seat and I'll bring it to your table."

This woman sank into the nearest chair, which was at my brother Swithin's small table. "Oh, hello," she said.

"Good afternoon," Swithin said.

"A cup of tea," she said, as though she were replying to a question. "That will be just the thing. A nice cup of tea." She was carrying a cloth satchel in one hand, and now she put it on the floor beside her. "Where is this? I've never been here before!"

A certain percentage of the customers at The Bohemian Pirate were people who had lost their way. They were tourists or even Londoners who had somehow got off their accustomed track. Swithin started to describe where they were, but she suddenly said, "I feel silly, in a way, but then what was I to do?"

"King Edward College is just around the corner from here," Swithin said helpfully. "I teach there, actually. It's quite a pleasant district, if a bit out of the way."

"Well," she said ruefully, "it is certainly out of my way!"

"The Tube station isn't very far," Swithin said. "Ten, maybe fifteen minutes."

"I'm more a bus person," she said.

"Buses go past the Tube station. You'll probably get your bearings there."

Fleur arrived with a pot of Earl Grey and a little tray with milk, sugar, and lemon slices. The woman looked briefly for a fork and then picked up two of the lemon slices and dropped them into the cup. Now she poured the aromatic tea into the cup and the lemon slices floated to the top and then sank again.

"It was ridiculous, really," the woman said.

"When you get on to the main road you'll soon see where you are. There are several buses."

"I've just come on one of them. I don't mind, really. I mean, I did it on purpose." She pressed down on the lemon slices with her spoon. "I've no one to blame but myself!" she said laughing a little.

Swithin was now more than a little perplexed about this grey-haired woman sitting opposite him who somehow seemed to have done something unwise and preventable and got lost, more or less intentionally. King Edward College wasn't in such an extravagantly obscure corner of London! Sometimes he wished people would stop insinuating that King Edward's location was peculiar and barely findable. It was true that it was an in-joke at the college: new students couldn't find it, prospective employees coming for interviews couldn't find it, and so on. But it wasn't the kind of joke that other people were supposed to think of first.

"You see," she said, "I wanted to get off at least five or six stops back, but I just couldn't."

Swithin thought she must have some disability he hadn't noticed at first. "Oh, I'm sorry!" he said.

The woman looked at him with some surprise. "Nothing to be sorry about!" she said briskly.

"I thought that perhaps you...I mean, was there some reason that you couldn't get off there? Was something preventing you?"

"Oh well, yes, in a way," she replied, taking a tentative sip of tea. "I was standing on the bus. There were no empty seats, so I was standing, but in a moment a young man noticed me and offered me his seat. It is rather a relief to find manners in the young, don't you think?"

Swithin was a little discomfited to think that he should be expected to agree about some quality of "the young", when he himself was barely thirty. On the other hand, some of his students were definitely "the young" and he found them painfully immature and unmannerly. But then it seemed that everybody in London of all possible ages and sexes put their feet up on the seats in the Underground and the suburban trains. He thought it was a relief to find manners in anybody.

"Yes," he said. "So this chap gave you his seat?"

"Yes, it was very kind of him. He was quite young. He may have still been in his teens. He was a sweet boy. He caught my eye and half rose out of his seat and gestured for me to come and sit down. It was something of a questioning gesture, as though asking me if I wanted to sit, and if so I could have his seat. He was quite eloquent even without saying anything!"

Swithin thought perhaps this was one other person who didn't put his feet on the Underground seats. He thought that in all of London they could probably be counted on the fingers of relatively few hands. "He was a very thoughtful chap," Swithin said.

"Of course, nowadays with my grey hair I often do get seats on buses, but you know, it's usually from foreign people! Girls and boys both, and very often they aren't English. They're from the Continent, or they're quite swarthy. It makes you despair a bit of the English when foreigners are more polite on the buses!"

"I'm glad you get a seat, especially if you have far to go," Swithin said.

"Yes, I have to say it happens fairly often, but you can't count on it. And then too, some buses don't have very many seats anyway. It's as though you're meant to stand."

"They can get more people on a bus if more of them are standing," Swithin remarked.

"And it's all right if you aren't going far," the woman said. "In fact, for short distances I don't mind standing, but sometimes people have shopping and they need to sit down. And the buses lurch about so."

It seemed to Swithin that she was getting into a general critique of London Transport, and, while he could have contributed his fair share to the topic, the unanswered question still niggled in the back of his mind. "But why did you have to go past your stop?" he asked.

"The young man. He had been so polite. I couldn't just get off so soon after he had offered me his seat. I felt I needed to sit there for a while. It would have been hardly worth it for him to be polite if I was about to get off anyway."

"So you came on here out of your way?"

"Yes. I felt it was the only thing I could do."

"But the young man would have understood if you had got off at the right stop. He wasn't to know that you didn't need the seat for very long."

"You may be right, but I felt that this kind young man might think twice before offering his seat again if he thought that I didn't really need it. The next time he might think, 'There's a grey-haired old lady, but if I give her my seat she may not really need it anyway; she may be getting off soon.'"

"I understand your point," Swithin said. "But surely the young man—or woman—would just see someone in need of a seat and not think how long they were going to sit in it. I think I myself would give up my own seat on a bus and not think of that. There's no way to know how long..."

"You are obviously one of the polite ones!" the woman exclaimed with a smile. "But for someone who isn't used to being polite, who might be still learning how to do it, don't you think that it is important for him to see the value of his politeness? Well, that's what I thought, anyway. I was sitting there thinking, 'I must get off soon, but then this nice young man will notice and he might feel a little hurt.' So I went on past the next stop and the next."

"Was he watching you to see when you would get off?"

"No, not at all. In fact, he turned his back. I think that was another part of his politeness. He didn't want to look at me in case I would feel that I had to thank him again or keep looking grateful, so he politely turned aside."

"Maybe he wouldn't have noticed when you got off."

"I'm sure he would have noticed, though, and that's what kept me in my seat. I just couldn't bear to get off the bus and perhaps disappoint that kind young man!"

Swithin could see that it was an awkward impasse. He hadn't thought of the subtleties of the matter before. He offered his seat now and then, but thought no more about it. "But then you finally got up the resolve to get off this bus anyway?"

"Yes," she said ruefully, "but that was only because the young man had already got off. I couldn't bear to get off before that. It's a bit silly, isn't it?"

"No," said Swithin, but he privately thought the woman was being too fastidious about it. "But frankly, the next time it happens it would probably be safe to get off at your intended stop. I feel sure that the polite person who had given you his seat would understand and not hold it against you."

"You really think so?"

"Yes, really. I would think no more about it if I were you."

"Very well. You have put my mind at rest!" She had finished her tea now and taken the weight off her feet and was ready to go again. She stood up, picked up her things and turned to go. "Thank you very much, young man," she said. "You often give up your seat to people who need it more, don't you?"

Swithin was startled by her sudden accusation. "I...well, yes, of course. It's only the right thing to do."

"I thought so," she said. "I could see it. Good-bye now, and thanks."

Swithin returned to his work, unsure what she had thanked him for.

THE CRIME OF BEAUFORT SIMMONS

My brother Swithin used to say that he was deeply puzzled about Beaufort Simmons. He had been plainly nervous when he saw the two policemen in The Bohemian Pirate, but why? He was obviously an honest, hard-working man who should have nothing to fear from the law. Beaufort Simmons was black, of course, and Swithin wondered if that was part of it. Beaufort would occasionally come into The Bohemian Pirate, but it was always a brief visit and usually on business. There was a job of plaster patching to be done in the utility room and Beaufort promised to do it when he had a gap in one of the College jobs.

One day Swithin said to Ronan as he was getting his first cup of coffee, "Your friend Beaufort, have you known him for a long time?"

"Quite a long time. He did some work in a theatre we were involved with. The manager and the lighting designer both liked him a lot. Then when we had some work for him here, we were lucky to get him."

"So he's quite busy, is he?" Swithin asked.

"Oh yes!" Ronan said. "You have to get on his books, like an agent. He has jobs all over the place. He does council jobs – quite a lot for Lambeth and

Southwark. He's formed a company now and employs ten or fifteen other men. He's very capable and very reliable. You need him for something?"

"No," Swithin said. "Not really. I was just curious. Just wondered."

"His team – it's like a team – does some work for Barclays Bank, in their branches, when they're doing them up. Beaufort usually does the plastering himself, and then one of his mates does the redecorating."

"He seems very successful," Swithin observed.

"He deserves to be! He works like a dog, but he loves it. He really does. When he comes to do whatever it is – installing lights, plastering a wall – you get the impression there's nothing he'd rather be doing. Some blokes come in and give you the impression there are hundreds of things they'd rather be doing. Not Beaufort. He's one in a million!"

This extravagant praise for Beaufort Simmons puzzled Swithin all the more. He finally decided that Beaufort's nervousness about the police must just go back to some unfortunate incident in his youth. Perhaps he had got in with the wrong group of youngsters and the police had cautioned them. It might be nothing more than that.

The day came when Beaufort arrived to do the job in the utility room. Between applying layers of plaster Beaufort had to wait for a while and Ronan managed to persuade him to sit down and have a cup of coffee and a slice of cheesecake.

Swithin was pleased when he came to sit at his table because he wanted to talk to him. Soon he was telling Swithin about his family back home and his daughter, Alice, who lived with him.

"That girl!" he laughed. "She the best thing ever happen to me! Her mama wasn't the best thing for me, but my Alice, she sure is!"

Alice was a girl of 12 and had everything her hard-working father could give her in addition to the unbuyable gift of a doting dad. The girl had been handed over to him as a baby when the child's mother had decided motherhood wasn't her bag.

"My mama look after her when she was a tiny little baby. My mama didn't have no use for Alice's mama. She used to say to me, 'Beaufort, that girl of yours is no more use than a banana seed!' She used to call her that. Not to her face, but at home. 'That banana seed of yours,' she'd say. But I did not like Alice to hear her talk like that. Alice need to have some respect for her own mama. We come here when Alice was five. Just me and Alice, making a life of our own. Then my sister come. She help with Alice and it good for Alice to have her auntie to talk to. She going to be a young woman someday soon."

Then Beaufort had to go back and check on his plaster and add the final smooth finish.

"He's a perfectionist," Ronan said.

But after Beaufort left, Ronan told Swithin a disturbing thing: Beaufort had to be off work the following week because he had to appear in a magistrate's court.

"You mean as a witness?" Swithin asked.

95

"No, it's serious. He's being charged with something. I can't believe he's guilty of anything! I just don't believe it. He doesn't say much about it, but he just told me he'd be away from work next Wednesday."

"You could always go to the magistrate's court yourself and see what it's all about. You could even put in a good word for him if he needs a character reference."

"Could I do that?" Ronan asked. "Just walk in?"

"Of course," Swithin said. "Those courts are always open to the public. Anyone can go."

"I think he's embarrassed about the whole thing. He might not want anybody he knows to be there."

"But that presupposes that he has done something wrong or illegal, and you don't think he has done. I'm inclined to agree with you."

"All right, I'll go. Eh, Swithin, while I'm gone, I mean, I'll be away from the café here for a few hours probably, so could you, do you think you could..."

"No problem, Ronan. I can help out again. I can do the till, and I can make four kinds of coffee, not counting filter. You go and tell them that Beaufort is an honest man and a responsible father."

"Right! I'll go!"

"Maybe there's been a mistake," Swithin said.

"I wouldn't be surprised. Mistaken identity. You know, frankly, these cops, they can't always tell one black person from another, can they? I mean, look at some of these cases that come up."

"Times when a black person is falsely accused of something and then it emerges that the police have been racially prejudiced?" Swithin suggested.

"Exactly!" said Ronan. "They get prosecuted, they get sent to prison, and later they find out that it was all a mistake. We can't let that happen to Beaufort!"

The next afternoon Beaufort came into The Bohemian Pirate for a few minutes between jobs. He had to hurry off to another part of London to get a plastering job started. "That way," he said, "I can finish it tomorrow, right? The travelling take up a lot of time. It going to take more time than the job itself! The time I spend on the road between jobs!"

"Beaufort," Swithin said, "I heard about this...this visit to the magistrate's court, and..."

"Oh that!" Beaufort said. "I made a big mistake! I just hope that court don't take it too serious!"

"Well," Swithin said, "we all make mistakes. Everybody..."

"Yeah, well I sure done the wrong thing, and right there in Parliament Square! That cop wrote down my registration number, want my address, everything. When I realize what going on, it too late! I made one big mistake, I tell you!"

Beaufort didn't seem to want to go into more detail, and he was in too much of a hurry even to drink the coffee–or orange juice–he was offered. When he had left, Swithin went to the counter to speak to Ronan.

"Ronan, he just told me he was stopped by the police in Parliament Square for doing something wrong. Maybe it was a traffic violation of some kind. He said he did the wrong thing. Maybe he tried to make a right turn out of Whitehall."

"No," Ronan said. "I asked him if it was to do with traffic or his road tax disk and he just groaned and said it wasn't. But the cops did stop his van, I got that out of him."

"So maybe they were actively looking for him. Is that possible?"

"Anything's possible," Ronan said glumly. "But whatever he's supposed to have done, I think he's innocent."

"But he said he made a mistake and he did something wrong – both statements suggestive of a confession. He must have done something – he says so himself."

"Yes, it seems so," Ronan admitted.

"Theft? Fraud? Tax evasion?"

"But you can't do that in a van in Parliament Square, and that's where he said he did something wrong."

"Yes," said Swithin. "It doesn't make sense, does it?"

In the days before the court appearance Swithin often found himself wondering what this conscientious builder and devoted father could have done to attract the attention of the police. Swithin and Ronan had exhausted all avenues of speculation and kept the conversation on other subjects when they spoke to each other in The Bohemian Pirate. Still, they each privately vacillated between being sure that Beaufort was innocent of whatever he was charged with and wondering what he could have done that caused the police to run him in.

INSPIRATION

My brother Swithin was apparently winding up one of his chapters, just getting to the part where he was going to leave a space and then compose a few paragraphs of "Conclusion", drawing together all the points he had been making in that chapter. Since his office and the whole hallway were still full of building noise, ladders, tarpaulins, satchels of tools, workmen in overalls, and cables lying around everywhere, he was over at The Bohemian Pirate. He didn't have a laptop yet. He just had old-fashioned notebooks and his favourite clipboard and his file cards. He had a particular blue pen—I mean a pen with blue ink—that he liked and another red one for corrections and scribbles in the margin.

Keith operated the Gaggia machine and handed Swithin his cup of coffee. Later he would get further cups and the odd sandwich. That was pretty much Swithin for the day.

So he drafted his conclusion on a pad of lined paper, and then later Elspeth in the office would type it up. She had learned to read his sloppy handwriting. It was beyond most people. Fortunately when Swithin went to California and then Chicago he always typed his letters. And then eventually there was e-mail.

Maybe this fellow just coming through the doorway had some business at the College. It was hard to see how any non-Londoner could have found The Bohemian Pirate otherwise, although of course they did wander in from time to time. He sat down at Swithin's table. Swithin looked around as though to indicate his surprise that the stranger hadn't chosen another table. The fellow just sat looking down at his lap and sighing. Keith asked him if he wanted coffee.

"Yes," said the man, whose name was Jankovic. "Coffee. Whatever. With milk. With milk and sugar. I'll put it in myself." His English was accented but not hard to understand.

The actor went away and now Jankovic looked blankly at Swithin's papers taking up all his side of the table and more. "You're a writer," he said. "Do you write fiction?"

Swithin told him it was not fiction.

"No, of course not," said the other. "Who would write fiction? Who would bother?"

His tone of voice made Swithin look up. What was the man talking about?

"I write fiction, actually," he said. "My name is Arno Jankovic. You have never heard of me, I know. I have written some novels. It is true that they are unpublished, but that does not really detract from the quality of the novel itself, does it? Nobody wanted to publish my novels," he added bitterly. "Now I will be forgotten."

"What happened?" Swithin asked, resigning himself to an answer.

"No one is buying novels now. Even if my novels were published, no one would buy them. No one in my country. The bottom fell away from that market."

"I see," said Swithin, wondering if some of the argument in his current chapter really belonged in the previous chapter. He could insert it in the middle section and then refer to it in the concluding paragraph.

"You are wise to write non-fiction," the central European said. "Very wise. The bottom will not fall away from that market. People will read non-fiction."

"I suppose some people will always read fiction," said Swithin. "Short stories, novels."

"Not in my country!"

"Why not?"

"Just think. Nothing is stranger or more inventive than the events every day in my country. How can I compete with reality? If people want a bizarre story, they have only to look in their newspaper. You can't invent those things! Maybe a genius. Maybe Shakespeare."

Swithin hardly knew what advice to give the man, or whether to offer any at all. He usually advised his students to plough on regardless. Keep going, keep at it, try again–all that kind of thing. You'll succeed eventually, don't give up heart – like that. Now he just said, "Perhaps these things go in cycles. Maybe tastes will change again."

"When? When I'm dead! In fifty years! By then my books—even if they were published—would be old and out-of-date and forgotten. Even if somebody published them. I write very good novels – very subtle. My mother likes them enormously. Not much happens in them in an obvious way. They are very intellectual in content. They are not cheap thrillers. They are not like this rubbish everyone reads here. And now look what's happened! I've sent my manuscript to five different publishers and they have all said that they aren't publishing any more novels for the time being!

"And shall I tell you more? Writers, in the past they were treated very well. They had stipends from the state and good places to live. Everyone looked up at them. I might have gained admission to the Writers' Union. Then everyone would read my books! I would have had an audience. People would have liked my novels. They are thoughtful and artistic, not like these trashy love stories that they read in the West. Not these ridiculous spy stories that appeal to persons with the lowest taste. Oh no, they are high quality."

Swithin was probably glazing over by now, if I know Swithin. When people tell him how good they are his patience is not so much thin as invisible. Before he could say, "Well, well" or "Bad luck" or something, the man went on: "And do you know what else? I might have got them translated. I might have found a translator, and then they might have been famous world-wide, my stories. They could have appeared in some important literary journal abroad. I might have been famous!" Swithin looked down at his clipboard, where he was on page 32. He numbered all the chapters separately, at least at this draft stage.

Jankovic looked down, too, at the floor of The Bohemian Pirate. "I might have had a career," he said. "I could have been a success." He looked back at Swithin. "But now – now! Now I am somebody whose life is finished!"

Swithin was alarmed to see that the man was near tears. He looked around to see if anyone was watching, but there was no one else in The Bohemian Pirate at that hour.

"Look," said Swithin. "I mean, cheer up. It can't be as bad as all that. Something will turn up."

"You English are so optimistic!" Jankovic exclaimed bitterly. "Everything will be all right! But very often it is not all right. In my country things are very often not all right. Very often things turn out all wrong. In other countries you can afford to be optimistic because sometimes things work out. In my country only a madman would..."

The man seemed to be getting more dejected by the minute, and Swithin tried to change the subject. "Look, why don't you go and look for something to write about? Sit in a park or get on a bus or something. Some topic will no doubt occur to you. You will devise a plot, think of a fictional character, a set of characters. I'm sure you'll think of something." He knew it sounded lame, but the Balkan chap seemed to be about to have a nervous breakdown in front of him. "You can look at people and imagine their lives – or make up lives for them. That's what novelists do, isn't it?"

Jankovic was still looking glum. "Yes," he said. "I suppose so. I was almost in the Writers' Union. I was young and promising. That's what my mother said. She was a very good judge of literature."

"They say you should write about what you know." Swithin's advice was getting lamer all the time.

"What do I know? Everything I used to know has changed into something I do not know. Everything has changed. Everything is downside up!"

"Well," said Swithin. "Well, look. The thing is…"

"Wait!" Jankovic said. "I have an idea!"

"Good," said Swithin.

"I think I have an idea!"

Swithin looked down at his clipboard, still on page 32.

"I'm going to take your advice!"

Swithin tried to think which particular cliché might have appealed to the man.

"Yes! I think you've solved my problem!" There was a rather wild and exalted look in the man's eye and Swithin wondered if he'd just traded the depressive phase for the manic one.

"That's good," Swithin said.

"You've done it! We've done it together!" he exclaimed, retracting some of the credit he had impulsively given Swithin. "Yes, I think I see the way forward. I may be able to build up my reputation. Maybe no one will even notice. No one will ever know that I faltered! You will not tell."

Swithin wasn't sure whether he was assuming his honour or his stupidity. Either he would be discreet and not tell anyone or he wouldn't know who to tell anyway. "No," Swithin said.

"I'm going to start working on it today," the novelist said. "This very day!"

"Good," said Swithin.

"The preliminary part. Notes. I always make a lot of notes. I must think carefully about the setting. The background. That is always very important in my novels." He had turned back into the impressive man of letters.

"That's fine," said Swithin, glancing down at his clipboard with all the blank sheets of A4 under his page 32. "That's really fine. I'm so glad."

"I could set it here in London or in my home city. Or even somewhere else. I must consider this carefully."

"I'm glad you've solved your problem. I'm sure everything will be all right now. What are you going to do?"

"I'm going to write my most important novel to date." He seemed to be composing the blurb already. "It will be about a man – a writer, as a matter of fact – who is coming to terms with the great social and political changes in his country— in his former country. His problem – this is the interesting part – is that he has been writing successful novels (he's quite a famous novelist, in point of fact), but now suddenly fiction is no longer required. You see his dilemma, don't you? What is he to do? His quandary is a great universal quandary faced by the citizen of the modern world. The novel will have enormous resonance now and in the future. That is why I say it will be my most important work to date. My character –the hero of this ground-breaking novel–decides to write a novel, but about his own predicament. It is fiction, but it will be a kind of social document at the same time."

"Brilliant," said Swithin.

"It will create a whole new genre of prose fiction!" Jankovic said. "Some of our problems now are lucky problems. In former times we would have been glad to have such problems. I mean, problems about how to convey the truth of one's experience. Problems like that."

"Excellent," said Swithin. "Congratulations."

"Other novels will be compared to this one, but this will be the first of the genre, the standard against which others will be judged. It will be a landmark in modernity. When you see my new book–when it's translated–you can remember that you were my inspiration."

"Thank you," said Swithin, but the man Jankovic was already pushing his chair back and rising from the table. In a moment he had reached the door and was out of The Bohemian Pirate.

Swithin turned back to his clipboard, which was still in the same state it had been in an hour before. He asked Keith for a cappuccino and tried to get back to his train of thought about winding up his chapter. When you've just played such a pivotal role in modern–if not even post-modern–European literature, it's hard to concentrate on your own page 32, but cappuccino helps.

THE MUG BUYER

She sat down at Swithin's table without appearing to see him. Swithin thought she looked like an actress whose name he couldn't quite remember. A wholesome American who could run a cattle ranch or be glamorous in New York. And who was that male lead? It couldn't be Glenn Ford, could it? Not Alan Ladd. Gary Cooper? Possibly Gary Cooper. But who was that actress? Not Barbara Stanwyck, not June Allyson, or perhaps it was June Allyson. He was trying to remember the title of the film when the woman opposite him put her coffee cup down and sighed.

"I've bought another mug," she said, almost to herself. But to Swithin it was obvious that she had bought a cup of coffee, not a mug. He must have looked at her quizzically in spite of himself, what with her calling a cup a mug and him not remembering the name of the film that starred the actress who looked like her and whose name was on the tip of his tongue.

She took another sip of latte and came back down to earth enough to address Swithin directly. "I've bought a mug to take to school," she explained.

"Not a mug of coffee," Swithin said.

"A mug for coffee," she said. "In the staff room. Every year I get a new mug."

"To celebrate the new school year?" Swithin enquired politely.

"No," she said. "Not at all. God, no." She took another sip.

"I started this job exactly seventeen years ago. I teach English at a secondary school in Cricklewood. I've been out and about doing some shopping today and I got this mug." She took a lump of tissue paper out of a big shopping bag and unwrapped a mug and placed in on the table. It was what is called "cheap and cheerful".

"That's very nice," Swithin said.

"It was the tackiest-looking mug I could find," the teacher said.

"But it's..." Swithin said, finding himself oddly defensive.

"I always try to find a really cheap mug at the beginning of the school year. I'm always afraid I'll break a good one. Or it could disappear. You never know what might happen to it in the staff room. Other people use it, or it gets chipped or somebody chucks something on top of it in the sink. There's a little sink in the staff room."

This school sounded like a dangerous place to Swithin, and he wondered what the pupils were like. Were there any ex-pupils of this place at King Edward College, he wondered. "So you get an expendable mug every year just in case?"

"Yes," she said. "If I got a really good china mug I would always be worried that something would happen to it, and then I would be sorry if anything did happen to it."

"But," said Swithin, who was beginning to see a fallacy here, "you have already bought one at the beginning of each academic year. Have they all been destroyed or damaged?"

"Oh, no. In fact, I have them all."

"But why don't you use one of them this year? If you already have so many mugs and they're all…"

"But the whole point," she said, "is to take something to school that I wouldn't mind losing. After I've had a mug for a year, I get attached to it. I can't very well take it back the next year because I'd be afraid that something might happen to it."

"So you must have quite a collection of these expendable yet extant mugs?" Swithin enquired.

"Yes," she said with a sigh, "nothing ever does happen to them. Things happen to other people's mugs, but not to mine. They get lost, the handles get broken, somebody drops them on the floor. There's no carpet on the floor. It isn't that kind of school."

Swithin's own coffee break arrangements were taken care of either by Elspeth in the departmental office or at The Bohemian Pirate, especially now in the summer when almost the only people in College were men in overalls doing advanced research in painting and plastering and electrical engineering with special reference to three-pronged plugs. There were certain projects with ladders concerning gravity and angles of incline. There would be ample scope for dropping coffee mugs and breaking them.

"I don't have a special coffee mug, myself," said Swithin. "I don't think anybody does. There's some College crockery. I teach around the corner at King Edward. It's just heavy white cups and saucers. They don't even have the College crest on them. I suppose they get broken from time to time, but they all look the same."

"You're lucky," she said. "If something gets broken, they just replace it, I suppose, and nobody notices."

"Yes. They're all the same. It would be hard to become attached to any of it."

"Pity my school doesn't have something like that. The school governors would have a fit if we asked them to buy us mugs or cups and saucers. They'd say..."

They were interrupted by the voice of Beaufort Simmons, who had come in to have his tea flask filled with hot water. He was usually soft spoken, but now he was saying to Keith, "I don't know! I wish I did! I just don't know, you hear what I'm saying?"

Swithin was sure that the subject was not plastering or decorating or plumbing, because there was nothing Beaufort didn't know about those subjects.

"But they must have said something," Keith was saying. "They must have made a charge. Did they actually charge you with anything?"

"Police bail! They give me police bail! They think I a criminal! They only criminals get bail."

"And the innocent!" said Fleur loyally. "Bail doesn't mean you're guilty!"

111

"They could find me guilty!" Beaufort said. They say, 'Look that black guy he prob'ly guilty, we go ahead, send him down,' and there go my work, my business, everything, right down the tubes!"

"But Beaufort," Fleur said, "what do they think you've done?"

"I was at Parliament Square, girl! They very touchy about that! Mother of Parliaments and all that! They just grab me!" Beaufort was more upset than Swithin had ever seen him. Beaufort, in fact, never seemed to be upset about much anything. He was a cheerful, confident man, good at his job and, as far as one could tell, with a happy family life. Had the police been influenced by the man's dreadlocks and chocolate-dark skin? Swithin thought it highly likely.

Swithin had completely lost the thread of his conversation with the teacher who bought mugs. He was thinking about poor Beaufort, who had been arrested but yet couldn't have done anything wrong, and about some references he would have to check at the British Library, but he felt that he should somehow address this woman's problem with her mugs.

"So," he said, "you have seventeen mugs now?"

"Eighteen, actually."

"Eighteen mugs. Quite a collection! Eighteen mugs that you have grown to like, although you bought them specifically so that you wouldn't care if they got broken."

"Yes. You've got it."

"Do you use them at home?"

"No, not much. They're too ugly and they don't match."

"But you can't just throw them out, give them to Oxfam, say?"

"I may have to eventually," she said resignedly.

"Maybe you could give them away as prizes," Swithin suggested, trying to think of something helpful.

"Prizes? To the kids? Mugs? What would they do with them?"

"Well, maybe the ones who are going on to university might like to have a start on equipment for their digs. They will need mugs eventually. It could be a little memento of their years at school. Or of the sixth form. Do you teach sixth form?"

"As a matter of fact, I do," the teacher said.

"Well, you could tell them that it was a pleasure having them in your class and here's a little something to remind them of happy days, eh, reading Wordsworth, and good luck at university. How's that?"

The teacher was quiet for a moment. "I hadn't thought of that before. I might give it a try. That would get rid of some of them. I couldn't give them all away at once, but if I gave one away every year I'd still have the same number, wouldn't I?"

"You could give two or three away at the same time. Or more. Four or five. For exam results."

"But they are too cheap and ugly to give away as prizes. And the tea stains..."

"The tea stains could be got off with something," Swithin said a bit vaguely. "They might regard a personal gift as a special object, overriding the actual quality of the thing itself. You could say, 'Here is this mug I have been using'—you wouldn't have to say that it was fifteen years ago—'and as a mark of encouragement I would like to present it to you.' Something like that. What do you think? It might work."

"It might," she said. "There are always a few every year that go on. I could do that. But then, what happens when I give them all away? That could happen in three years and I wouldn't have enough to keep doing it."

"You would have to buy some more," Swithin said. "In the end they would be bought as prizes rather than as the annual mug. Or you could obtain something that was a more suitable prize. A pen, for example, or a little plaque or certificate. You could cross that bridge when you come to it."

"I could give the mugs away, find good homes for them," the teacher said.

"Yes, find good homes for them. They would be used again, and they would be a meaningful gift."

"I could get rid of them and they would be a meaningful gift," she repeated.

Swithin was watching Beaufort Simmons but trying not to let the teacher see that he wasn't giving her his full attention. Beaufort was leaving The Bohemian Pirate in an uncharacteristic slouching posture, and Swithin found that he was a little worried about him. Something seemed to be very wrong, but what could it be?

"Think you might try it?" Swithin asked politely.

"I just might, but I'll have to wait until the end of the summer term next year."

"You have all that time to plan precisely how you will do it."

"Well!" she said, brightening up. "You've been an enormous help! Thank you very much! What do you do at King Edward? Are you the student counsellor there? You'd make a good one!"

Swithin knew how to take compliments, except when they came unexpectedly. "No, I'm a lecturer. But sometimes I have to advise my students."

"Suppose I present you with a mug as a token of my thanks?" the teacher asked. "I could give you quite a colourful one with poppies on."

"That's very kind of you," said Swithin. "I appreciate your thoughtfulness, but I mustn't deprive some student of yours of his potential prize. Or her prize," he added quickly.

"No," she said. "Quite right. I'll hang on to them all, for the time being anyway."

"They'll make wonderful prizes later."

"Yes indeed!" she said. "I'll start with the one with poppies on."

"Excellent!" Swithin said.

THE HOROSCOPE

The young man sat across from Swithin reading the afternoon paper with great attention. He wasn't looking at the front page, which seemed to be all about London bus fares, but was burrowing around in the back pages. Swithin looked up to see where all the rustling was coming from. He was about to look back at his clipboard, but just then the man spoke. "I don't know whether you believe in horoscopes," he said, and it was impossible to tell whether he meant it as a question or a statement.

As Swithin realized that he was being addressed, he gave a slight smile and a nod and went back to the chapter he was working on. But the man continued.

"I read the horoscopes, myself," he said. "I think there must be something to them." This man was younger than Swithin, early twenties perhaps, and Swithin wondered if he had seen him at King Edward College. He was sure he hadn't been in any of his classes. Swithin considered horoscopes complete nonsense.

"Oh yes?" he said noncommittally and looked down again by way of a hint.

"Well," said the man, "I might not have believed them except that they seem to be sort of true. I'm a Gemini, and practically everything this particular horoscope-casting person in the Express says is uncanny. I mean, it mostly really applies to me."

When Swithin heard this sort of thing he could go into a speech about statistics and psychology and then in the end even if you were a Gemini or something you could see that there couldn't be much to it. But on this occasion he didn't want to get into a long acrimonious conversation with this stranger at his table in The Bohemian Pirate.

"Well," said Swithin.

"I mean, all the time. Day in day out. Every day I read my horoscope and it says, you know, more or less what is really happening in my life. Like, things will be tough in the middle of the week but get better a day or two later. Or financial matters will be important on Monday. All that sort of thing. Or Jupiter is moving into my sign, and..."

"That's very," said Swithin, "interesting. Very useful." And he looked down again, but it was no use.

"What's your sign?" the man asked, and it was nearly too much for Swithin.

"I really don't know," he said, controlling himself and speaking in a slightly clipped way. Swithin would never have been actually rude to this stranger, but all the same the man was on thin ice.

"Well, when were you born and I'll tell you."

But the last thing that Swithin wanted to know was his astrological birth sign. "I think it's...Capricorn, actually." He said the first thing that came into his head.

"Oh well, Capricorn. It says here that you must be careful of your health just now and avoid stress."

Swithin mentally rolled his eyes. "That sounds like good advice for any day of the week."

Since his concentration had been broken by this fellow, he caught Ronan's eye and made a little gesture that meant, "Another latte, please."

"So these predictions come true, do they?" he asked, trying to sound civil and interested.

"Oh yeah, most of the time, like I said. I don't know how she does it. There must be something in it."

"So have you been reading your horoscope for a long time?"

"Not all that long. For the last year or two. About a year and a half. But in all that time, on the whole, they've been more or less spot on."

More or less spot on, Swithin thought, whatever that meant. "I see," he said.

"Actually, the horoscope I read most is my sister's. That's Pisces."

"And then you pass on the news to her?" Swithin asked.

"Well, no," the young man said. "I can't do that."

"Why is that? Doesn't she believe in horoscopes?"

"No, I mean that's not the reason. She...she's...she died."

"Oh, I'm sorry," Swithin said automatically, and he really was. The young man suddenly looked sad and vulnerable.

118

"I got started doing it," he said, "around the time my sister died. I would look to see what her horoscope would have been if she had lived."

"But if she wasn't alive, how…"

"I just wanted to see how things might have been for her if she hadn't died when she did. Later on she might have had happiness and success and everything."

"Was you sister younger than you?" Swithin asked.

"Yes, she was only nineteen when she died. That's no age, is it? She had her whole life…" the man looked as though he might cry. Swithin was always terrified of people crying in front of him. This guy certainly had not been sent by the horoscope if Swithin was supposed to avoid stress. "She had her whole life," he repeated, "before her."

"That's too bad," Swithin said. "We had a student at King Edward who died last year. He fell down a mountain in Wales during the summer vacation. When the new term took up there was a kind of sadness in his year. The news got round during the first few days."

"But my sister shouldn't have died. She should still be alive now. She could be sitting here with us!"

"What happened to your sister?"

"My sister—her name was Marie—she decided one day to kill herself." He said it as though he hadn't said these words very much before. They sounded new and rough on his tongue. "She was feeling depressed. We didn't notice anything special. In fact, she seemed quite cheerful just before...just before she did it. She had been in a funk and then she cheered up, but then she did it anyway."

"But her horoscope..."

"I like to read her horoscope because I can kid myself that she's still alive. And because I can see whether, if only she'd stuck it out, she might have come through it, might have had something good happen in her life."

"Is that a comfort to you?"

It is, in a way. I haven't mentioned it to Mum and Dad. I don't know whether it would work with them. They're very...they're not the type."

"So she lives on in her horoscope?" Swithin asked gently.

"Yeah. I read about Pisces and I think that she could still be watching her health or financial matters or having a pleasant surprise from someone near her. Things like that."

"How are things going with Pisces people now?" Swithin asked.

"Better. For a while there things weren't so good. Just after she died, it was all pretty bad. There were reversals at work and difficult matters that had to be confronted."

"Had she had reversals at work and so on?"

"I don't know. I don't think so. She was just kind of sorrowful. She had just broken up with her boyfriend, but I don't think that was it, either. It wasn't any particular thing, as far as I know. Maybe there really were difficult matters to confront or a loved one who presents problems. We never knew and she didn't leave a note."

"She didn't give you any clue about how she was feeling?"

"No. She just took an overdose. She took a whole bottle of these pills. That day the horoscope said, 'You are feeling low at the moment but it won't last'. Well, it didn't last, but do you think that's what the horoscope woman meant? I thought at the time that I might write and ask her, but there was other stuff to do."

"Perhaps," said Swithin, "she wouldn't have known anyway, if the horoscope was meant in a general way for all the people who might read it. She might not have been able to tell you anything important."

"No, that's right. But it was spot on, wasn't it? So I kept reading it, like an addiction. Every day I would read what she might have had in her life. For a long time it wasn't very good. Pisces types were having a really rough time. Their finances were difficult and their romantic life took a turn for the worse and their work colleagues caused friction. I kept thinking of her having all those problems, and I would feel really sorry for her, and then I would remember that she wasn't having those problems after all. But then I would feel sorry all over again, because it would really be preferable to have those horoscope problems than not...not to have anything."

"But then things got better, you were saying?"

"Yeah, after a while. Like now, things are really looking up. Mercury is in her sign or something. Or Venus. Something is in her sign and it's all go. But she died a year ago last February, so she's not...she's not..."

"It doesn't apply to her," Swithin said.

"Right. None of that applies to her now."

Swithin almost didn't mind it that this conversation was about fortune-telling columns in the popular press.

"But," said the girl's brother, "it might have applied to her. If she had just stuck it out. You hear that people who...take overdoses don't really mean it. They don't always. It says here that by the end of the week her spirits will lift. Or rather, Pisces' spirits will lift. Now you see, she could be happy now! She would be through the friction with the workmates and all that, whatever it was that was making her unhappy. If she just hadn't messed up like that."

Swithin thought about what might have been in the life of this girl and her sad brother. She was gone and the poor chap was looking for her in horoscope columns! She had indeed "messed up".

"It says here that there will be a new love interest. She's missing all this! She didn't know what she was going to miss."

"One's life," Swithin said, trying not to sound pompous, "one's life has various ups and downs. She would have gone on to have ups and downs in later years. It might not be spirits lifting and love interest all the time, you know. No doubt there was some underlying trouble, some sort of depression."

"Yeah, depression."

Swithin thought of the infinite possibilities of life, hardly hinted at in newspaper horoscope columns.

The little paragraphs didn't begin to scratch the surface. He had never heard of them being a cure for grief before. When would this chap ever stop reading his sister's horoscope? Now it was making Swithin sad.

"Can I get you a cup of coffee?" Swithin asked.

"Thanks. Then I've got to go. It was nice to talk to you. I can't talk to my parents about this. They would think it was weird or something."

"No, it's not weird," Swithin said decisively. "Not if it takes some of the pain away. You have to deal with it however you can. Maybe later on you can stop reading them. Read your own if you want to, but I mean maybe you can stop reading your sister's."

"I should probably stop reading hers eventually, shouldn't I? She's not doing any of this stuff, the romantic interest and all that. She doesn't have the financial problems that will ease up on Wednesday, does she?"

"No," Swithin replied. "She doesn't have any of those things. They don't apply any more, if they ever did." He was sorry as soon as he had said that last part casting doubt on the principle of horoscopes, but the young man didn't seem to notice.

"My sister is dead," the young man said. "It was nice having a sister, you know. I would talk about Maric, I would say, 'My sister says'...or I would say, 'My sister and I'. We got along really well. We used to tell each other stuff. And now I don't have a sister anymore."

"You don't have any other..."

"No, it was just the two of us. It really killed my parents. Not literally! I mean they were really knocked out by it. They still can't think about anything else."

"I'm sure that time will heal..."

"Yeah, time," the man said. He had heard it all before. "Time takes care of it. It's early days yet. A year and a half is still early days, isn't it?"

"Yes," said Swithin, "it's early days."

The next time I saw my brother Swithin he was unusually sweet to me. It was Sunday lunch at our parents'. I accidentally dropped a little radio of his and broke it, and he didn't say anything. He just smiled and shook his head and that was all. He even gave me a little hug!

AN UNEXPECTED VISIT

Swithin looked up to see a woman outside the café taking a picture of it. She was a woman of a certain age (although she would not have phrased it so coyly herself) with short grey-ish hair. She wore brown corduroy trousers and a tan suede jacket with a pale green blouse and a flowing silk scarf, for it had suddenly turned cool. After she had taken a few more pictures from different angles, she came into the café. She looked around and seemed to be counting the tables. Swithin wondered if she was some sort of inspector sent out by the Council to check up on the "amenities on the public highway" and things like that. She was standing at the counter now, talking to Fleur. Swithin heard her ask for a decaffeinated cappuccino.

The woman took her cappuccino and sat down at a table next to Swithin's. She put her camera on the table and took out a small A5 folder and clipboard and began to write in it, waiting for her coffee to cool. Now and then she spooned up a bit of the chocolaty froth on top. Swithin tried to get on with the draft of chapter nine, but he felt that this other customer was staring at him and especially at his own clipboard and the box of notes in front of him. Finally he decided to speak.

"I saw you taking pictures of the café," he said. "Is it so remarkable?" He smiled in a somewhat conspiratorial way, as though they would both agree that it was nothing special.

The newcomer smiled back. "I want to remember the look of the outside of The Bohemian Pirate. I like the new awning. It's just the thing for this place."

"It is new, but how did you know that? I haven't seen you in here before."

"Oh, I'm very familiar with this place! For example, your name is Swithin. And it was Ronan who insisted on the awning. And you were rather taken with that blonde Dutch woman."

Swithin felt suddenly flustered. "That's all quite true!" He stared at the woman for a moment. "Oh, great heavens! Are you Sarah Lawson?"

"Yes," I said, "I am."

"I wasn't expecting you! I mean, of course we get all sorts, I mean, a lot of people come in here, but I somehow thought, you know, I rather imagined that you...that you..."

"That I wouldn't make an appearance in my own story?" I finished for him.

"Yes. That's what took me by surprise."

"Well, I wanted to see the place up close. I've spent months thinking about it. It's a nice café, isn't it?"

"Yes, indeed! I like it enormously."

"You don't have to say that just to please me," I told him.

"No, really. Anyway, I do have to say what you want me to say. Don't deny it."

"No, all right. You're right, Swithin."

"Tell me, Dr. Lawson, will I ever finish this book? I mean...all these interruptions...you're not making it easy for me."

"Please," I said, "call me Sarah. Well, you could finish it, although not on my time. Not in this book. But later – why not?" I looked down at my camera sitting on the table, a Canon SLR with a neck strap. It had several pictures left on the roll. Those were pre-digital days.

"I've got as far as chapter nine and I should really like to see it through to the end. I think I could find a publisher. I was thinking of Simnel and Warbeck."

"I'm sure you could find a publisher!" I said encouragingly. "I think Simnel and Warbeck has been bought by Random House. But never mind, you could do anything you like! Go for it! But not in my novel. Your job is to sit here in this café and observe things. Hear people's stories. Tell your sister about them. By all means tell her, because she is my narrator. When you finish with that, Swithin, the world is your oyster!"

"I've never liked oysters."

"Swithin," I said sharply, "don't get smart with me!"

"Sorry. But couldn't the world be my breaded scampi?"

"Whatever, Swithin. After my novel ends, you can write your own scenario."

Fleur came over to my table then; she had heard our conversation.

"Welcome to the Bohemian Pirate!" she said to me. "What an unexpected surprise this is!"

"If it's a surprise, naturally it's unexpected," I reminded her. "That's a tautology."

"Well," Fleur returned spiritedly, "whose fault is that?"

"Yes, touché, quite right."

"Like none of that's tautological, either."

"All right, you've made your point."

"So do you like the coffee? It's a dark roast Arabica, but without caffeine."

"Yes, thanks. It's excellent. Sometimes they seem to make milky coffee with any old thing and call it cappuccino."

"We never do that!" she said.

"I know you don't. The coffee here is really excellent, whatever the Tsolikides' upstairs may say," I replied.

"Yes, I agree," Swithin put in. "That's one reason I come here. That and the space. There's always a free table. I can get on with my book–when I'm not interrupted." He shot me a meaningful glance.

I ignored him. "I really meant to drop in very unobtrusively. I was trying to be just one of the anonymous customers."

Now Ronan appeared from the little kitchen and office through the door marked "Staff Only". "Look who's here!" Fleur said. "This is Sarah Lawson!"

"No kidding!" said Ronan. "Very pleased to meet you."

We shook hands. I was a little embarrassed by all the attention.

"Keith's gone for an audition, you know," he said.

"I know."

"He'll be sorry he missed you."

"You can tell him from me that he'll get a big part, but later."

"Later?" Ronan said.

"I mean after this novel. He can do it on his own time. He can do anything! The world's his..." I saw Swithin looking at me attentively. "...seafood," I finished. "You can all accomplish anything you want. A bit later."

"So The Bohemian Pirate will be a success?" Fleur asked.

"Oh yes," I said. "No doubt about it! Good coffee like this deserves success. And those muffins. As far as I'm concerned, you could skip the scones. You could drop the scones!"

They ignored my pun. I wasn't even sure they caught it. "But," said Fleur, "the customers like them."

"Well, keep them then," I said. "I don't mind. And keep having that good dark-roast decaf made with beans. Sumatra Rich Blend, I believe. Just because people don't want caffeine doesn't mean they don't want flavour! In some coffee shops they seem to think..." but before I could get really going on that hobby-horse Fleur interrupted.

"You know," Fleur said, "this place isn't so easy to find. You've really tucked it away."

"Yes," I said. "I did that on purpose. Actually, I walked right past the entrance to this little courtyard place the first time, myself! I didn't want people to know exactly where it was."

"Why was that?"

"Well, it was part of the invention–part of the way I imagined it. It's near this college, but then London is dotted with colleges. Just when you think you're in some obscure part of London, there's Royal Holloway or Goldsmith's. So it could be practically anywhere."

"It's fairly central, though."

"Yes," I agreed. "I think it's pretty central. In fact, it's not near Royal Holloway or Goldsmith's."

"It's near King Edward's," Fleur said dryly.

"Right. King Edward's College is just around the corner."

"Except that it's not on the A to Z."

"That's because unfortunately it is in the crack between pages. It's in the gutter, so that even if you open the A to Z flat it's still hard to find. That's often the case, isn't it? The place you want to go is always between pages, or if it's a folded map, it's exactly on the fold."

"All right, but the point is that nobody knows where this place is. You haven't explained it clearly, and now you say that was by design. Don't you want people to find The Bohemian Pirate? Don't you think we could do with the publicity? I mean, look at this little mews type place! If we get any passing trade it's only because people have got totally lost and are looking for something else!"

"It's not so bad in term time. You do quite a roaring trade on some days."

"Well, we have our faithful customers, like Swithin here, but we wouldn't mind some new customers now and then!   Proper customers, I mean, and not just these odd bods who wander in."

"I wouldn't call them 'odd bods'. They have interesting lives, like anybody else. But you think I should come right out and say that it's in Cockaigne Place?"

"Why not? They'll still have a job finding it."

"You could always advertise in *Time Out.*"

"We've already thought of that, but we'd appreciate anything you might do to help."

"Or perhaps some other street name," I mused. "Something a little more…"

"You've already been quite clever enough landing us with 'The Bohemian Pirate' in the first place!" Fleur exclaimed. "You and your droll Shakespearean references! The Bohemian seacoast! Actually, I played Hermione in *The Winter's Tale* once, you know. Little place in Bounds Green. Tiny stage."

"But that was your idea," I said. "You're resting actors. It was your little joke."

"Oh no it wasn't! It was all your idea and you know it. If it had been down to me I would have put up chintz café curtains and called it something cosy and welcoming, like 'So-and-so's Pantry' or 'The Coffeepot'."

"You wouldn't have done anything so corny!"

"I might have! If I'd been allowed to! But I wasn't, was I?"

I could see that we had reached a raw nerve here. I didn't see what I could do about it, though. A moment before when she was being so disrespectful I had thought of curtailing her acting career, but now I didn't have the heart to do it.

"But look," I said, "later when you're all successful actors you'll be selling this place anyway, won't you? So it's not like it's a millstone around your necks forever, is it?"

"We're going to be successful actors?" Fleur said, brightening up.

"Well, of course. You're just resting now, remember?"

"Successful," she said. "When do I get my big break-through? What role?"

"What would you like?"

"Ibsen perhaps. Something classical, maybe foreign. Maybe Chekhov. No, Ibsen. Ibsen, please?"

"Ibsen it is!" I said, happy to lighten her spirits. "How about Nora in *The Doll's House*"?

"I'd love that!" Fleur said. "How did you know?"

"Just guessed."

Fleur went back into the other room hesitantly, as though sorry to leave but wanting to get away before I changed my mind.

Ronan had been listening and seemed to take heart from the upturn in the conversation. "About these tablecloths..." he began.

"There are no tablecloths, Ronan," I said sharply. "Don't get carried away. You don't need tablecloths in The Bohemian Pirate. It's fine the way it is. It's a sort of coffeehouse. What do you think about calling it a coffeehouse?"

"I like 'coffeehouse'," Ronan said meekly. "I hope you don't think it's a 'caff'."

"Of course not. Not a bit of it! It's quite... it's rather...it's somewhat upmarket, really." I glanced at the little formica-topped tables. "These fine wooden tables, for example—beech aren't they? You ordered them through Heal's, I believe. No, this is a distinguished little coffee shop, and you'll go far with it. Even Starbuck's won't diminish your customer base."

"What are star bucks?"

"Never mind. It hasn't happened yet."

Ronan looked puzzled.

"The point is," I said, "that you've found your calling now. After all those years in drama school and that little run at the Marquis of Granby in Bounds Green..."

"Everybody has to start somewhere! Lawrence Olivier had to start somewhere! Richard Burton..."

"I understand," I said. "You're quite right. There's nothing wrong with The Marquis of Granby in Bounds Green. A bit grubby perhaps, and they play atrocious music, but the theatre upstairs is absolutely admirable. It's a fine little theatre with a good lighting system. People are happy to go out to the end of the Piccadilly Line to see those plays. It's an established fringe venue. Outer fringe, perhaps."

"Just fringe," Ronan said. "It's not at the end of the line—it's in zone 3, you know. There are four more stations and they're far apart. It's miles from the end of the line!"

"Fringe," I agreed. "It's a little fringe theatre. Perfectly respectable place. In the meantime you are also going to be a great coffeehouse proprietor, if you wish."

"Of course, we serve more than just coffee."

"Yes, there are those nice muffins. Blueberry muffins, chocolate chip, and the sandwiches."

"And the cakes and fruit tarts, the brownies, flapjacks, and..."

"Ronan, don't get carried away! You don't have any of those. Maybe later. See how it goes. The cheesecake is excellent, by the way, and you have apple strudel."

"OK, but we could expand things later."

I felt he was thinking, "...later, that is, when you get out of our hair!" but I didn't hold it against him. He can think what he likes.

I was about to finish my cappuccino and leave when Swithin spoke again. "So I am really going to finish this book? And get it published?"

"Oh, absolutely!" I said. "Unquestionably. You'll do King Edward College proud! Your scholarly reputation will grow and grow. You'll be a respected authority in your field, whatever it is. Don't worry."

"I was thinking," Swithin said quietly, "that I might move on, you know – that my career...well, I thought I might go and teach at an American university, perhaps."

"Why not?" I said. "Stanford maybe. How about the University of Chicago?"

"Oh yes! That would be ideal! I mean, either one."

"You have to apply first, obviously. Have you done that?"

"Not yet, but I was thinking about it. They advertise in the *Times Higher Education Supplement* and the *TLS*."

Well, do it," I said. "Frankly, I think you'll be successful. I'm sure of it. You probably wouldn't have to write in a café in those places." Fleur had come back out with a tray of excellent apple and cinnamon muffins, which she placed in the display case between an iced carrot cake and a tray of chocolate and walnut brownies. "Although," I added quickly for her benefit, "this is a splendid café. Or coffeehouse." Ronan was also within earshot.

"That's OK," said Fleur. "We know what you mean."

"Well, listen," I said. "I didn't mean to interrupt you here. I just wanted to have a look at the place."

"Even though you had trouble finding it?" Fleur said.

"Yes! I thought it was nearer the station."

"It's not near anything," said Ronan.

"Conversely," Swithin said, "you can get to it from almost anywhere."

"Almost?" I said. "Now Swithin..."

"Yes, all right," he said, smiling, "from anywhere at all."

"Keith will be sorry he missed you," Fleur said.

"Do give him my best when you see him," I said, picking up my camera and clipboard, and then I went out into Cockaigne Place and they lost sight of me.

Fleur turned to Swithin. "We should have asked her about Beaufort!" she said. "We could have

135

asked what this business is all about. She could have told us what's going on! Why didn't you ask her?"

"You could have asked her yourself," Ronan said.

"Of course, she might not have told us, even if we had thought to ask," Fleur said. "She's the type to keep you in suspense."

"Don't be too hard on her," said Swithin, still thinking about his future publishing and academic success. "We'll just have to wait."

BACKGROUND MUSIC

Swithin was at his usual place at The Bohemian Pirate, a latte in front him beside his clipboard and card file box. Engrossed in the introduction to a new chapter, he gradually became aware of the conversation at the counter. A young man seemed to be trying to sell Fleur something.

"Please think about it," he was saying. "Here's my card. Shall I come back later with some ideas for you? You have great potential here!"

Fleur thanked him for his card and said something that Swithin thought sounded noncommittal. She said she'd think about it and mention it to the others. Swithin wondered what this potential was and what Fleur was going to mention to Keith and Ronan.

The young man then asked for a cappuccino and a banana muffin, seeing that it was about time for elevenses, give or take an hour. Clutching his briefcase under one arm, taking the coffee cup in one hand and the plate with the muffin in the other hand and holding a spoon between his teeth like a pirate with a cutlass, he headed for the nearest table, which was Swithin's. Unable to say much with the spoon in his mouth, he put the cup and saucer and the plate down on Swithin's table, as there seemed to be plenty of room beyond the clipboard and file box.

"Mind if I sit here?" he said, sitting down.

Eh, no," Swithin replied. This was not an entirely true statement, but Swithin was a little curious to know what the young man was selling.

"Do you know the people here?" the man asked. "The people that run the place?"

"Yes," said Swithin. "They're friends of mine. They're all actors." He added loyally, "Very good actors. Their main interest is the stage." Now he was afraid he was being unjust to them in the other direction. "But their coffee is excellent! They are many-talented."

"I see," said the young man. "They probably like music, being actors."

"I suppose so. They can probably all sing if the part calls for it."

"They should care about the music in their shop, if they're at all sensitive to music or the atmosphere they want to establish."

"Music?" said Swithin. "There isn't any piped music here. It's nice and quiet."

"But think how nice it could be with some music! I mean appropriate music, of course. Nothing jarring. I don't mean raucous pop music or anything like that. Something soothing, maybe a little upmarket light jazz, maybe some light classics, opera overtures. It can enhance the atmosphere of an eating establishment simply immeasurably."

Swithin didn't care for the turn the conversation was taking. The last thing he wanted in The

Bohemian Pirate was muzak of whatever quality. He shuddered at the thought. "What did you have in mind for this place?" he asked.

"There is a real art to assessing just what kind of music would be appropriate here. Ideally I would drop in at different times of the day and sense the atmosphere, see what sort of people were here, that kind of thing. Maybe do a sampling of opinion. Then I could suggest some strategies."

"Do you advise a lot of clients on their background music?" Swithin asked.

"I'm building my business. I saw a gap in the market. One night my girlfriend and I were at a Chinese restaurant and they were playing some old hits by Splat. Do you know that group? No? It was a very youth thing a few years ago and then they started their own radio station, Splat Radio. You hear it everywhere."

Swithin had never heard it or heard of it and didn't even like hearing about it now. It sounded appalling.

"The point is," the young man went on, "that it was entirely wrong for this Chinese restaurant. It might have worked somewhere else. That's when I got the idea of advising restaurants and snack bars and so forth about their ambience. I do ethnic music for them. There's some terrific Chinese music out there! I got a tape of some zither type music for them. It brightened the whole place up. I told the guy it was like a fresh coat of paint and a new carpet!"

He needed your advice about Chinese music?" Swithin asked.

"Oh, yeah. He'd just never thought about it before. Some of these places, they just play whatever comes into their head. They don't think about the atmosphere they're creating. I try to get them to take some pride in their atmosphere, spend some time thinking about the impression they want to create, their signature, their individualised ambiance. Then they hire me to find the music for them and create the tapes. I take a good deal of pride in my work."

"Splendid," said Swithin.

"Yeah, I like my work. I built up this business myself. I'm still building it."

"How many clients do you have?" Swithin asked.

"Three. Well, this will be my third."

"But they haven't agreed yet."

No, but they could really improve this place with a little of the right kind of music."

"I'm afraid," Swithin said with as much regret as he could muster, "that they don't have much spare cash at the moment, for the foreseeable future. They're making some major purchases, I believe. They've bought some new furniture and they've had to buy a license from the Council. I'm afraid it is all running into a good deal of money."

"Oh," said the young man, and he seemed deep in thought.

Swithin also seemed to be thinking. "But you know," he said suddenly. "You know, there is another place not far from here that could really use your services!"

"Yes?" The young man brightened noticeably.

"Oh yes! It's on the other side of King Edward College. It is quite popular with the students, but it could be even more popular with your treatment. I'm sure they all listen to Splodge Radio."

"Splat."

"Indeed, 'Splat'. It may well be their favourite radio station. But I daresay they are quite eclectic. I'm sure they would appreciate any advice you could give them and perhaps order a tape or two."

"Where is this place?"

"It's called The Dispeptic Parrot and it's over in Bazalgette Parade, just two streets past the College." Swithin lowered his voice. "And I imagine they have the wherewithal to implement whatever you suggest. They do quite a trade there, I believe. It's well frequented by the students. The owner will probably be very keen to make improvements, keep up with the latest thing. I'm sure they care about their atmosphere and ambience."

The young man looked very interested. He took out the newest edition of the A-Z with a paperclip on the page for The Bohemian Pirate. He turned it so that he and Swithin could both look at it.

"Here we are," said Swithin, "and here's the College. Then here, you see, is Bazalgette Parade. Just here. It's a short street, and The Dispeptic Parrot is on the corner. You can't miss it. You can't miss their sign. Do you give advice about pub signs, by any chance?"

"I see where it is, yes, just round the corner. No, I don't do pub signs."

"Pity. As you say, it's practically round the corner from here. Five minutes, ten at the outside."

"I think I'll take your advice and pay them a visit! Can't hurt, can it?"

"No, indeed, it can't hurt. Perhaps you'll have another client! This would probably be a good time of day to see them. Later it may be rather crowded, but you could do your opinion research then."

The young man was gathering up his briefcase and putting the A-Z back in the outside pocket. "Good luck," Swithin said.

The young man finished his coffee quickly and made for the door. "Thanks," he called over his shoulder.

"Actually," Fleur said when she came to take the cup and muffin plate away, "we don't need any music here, do we, Swithin? I don't see Keith going for it, either."

"No, frankly, I don't think it would add anything. I like it the way it is."

"I'm glad to hear that. I do too. He seemed to be in a hurry."

"Yes, he's off to see another client. He had a sudden idea."

"Oh? Where's he going?"

"The Dispeptic Parrot," Swithin said.

"That place! He'll have to get them to play 'The 1812 Overture' at top volume and with real cannons, and even then they won't be able to hear it."

"It will certainly take all his genius and creativity."

"We've got enough on our plate here with Ronan's genius and creativity! First he ordered the tables and chairs, you know. The ones for outside.

And then he was determined to have that awning. Now he's angling for a ceiling fan."

"I heard about that," Swithin said. "Those are much sounder investments than a music tape, in my opinion."

"Too right," said Fleur, wiping the part of the table that wasn't claimed by Swithin's clipboard and file box. "I'll pass that on to Ronan."

THE LANDLADY

"You don't expect me to wear one of those?" Fleur said.

"No, of course not!" said Ronan. "Waiters wear them. Men. It's a male thing."

"It's pretentious, if you ask me."

"She's absolutely right!" Keith said. "Pretentious! I'm sorry, but you won't catch me wearing one of those aprons!"

"Ronan," Fleur said kindly, "honestly, it just doesn't fit here. This isn't Paris and this isn't a French bistro. Ronan, it's just not us, is it?"

"Ronan," said Keith, "if you want to fit the tone of the place, why don't you wear an eye patch? Or a red sash around your waist?"

"There's an idea!" Fleur exclaimed. "A red sash! That would suit you, too."

Ronan brightened up. "We could all wear red sashes!"

"Or it could be optional," Keith said, who was wearing a suit and tie and feeling a little overdressed.

"You know," Fleur said, as though changing the subject, "your idea for an awning was really good. I wasn't sure at first, but now I've come round to thinking it's just what we needed. It's a real improvement. Isn't it, Keith?"

"Awning yes, apron no," said Keith. "Hi, Swithin! Leave the door open, will you?"

Swithin had just come in, holding his briefcase and opening the door with his free hand. Now he pushed the door wide open until it clicked and stayed in place.

"Hello, all," he said. "I need a double latte when you have a moment. And perhaps a blueberry muffin."

"We have some new apple and cinnamon ones," Fleur said.

"Later," said Swithin. "That can be my second muffin. Perhaps my afternoon muffin."

"And we have some fantastic new lemon meringue pie!"

"I could have some of that, too."

"Don't go mad," Fleur said teasingly. "The book's coming along well, is it?"

"Very well!" Swithin said. "I can see the proverbial light at the end of the tunnel. I'm easily two-thirds into it. I've built up a certain momentum. Yes, it's coming along well! So I'll celebrate with a blueberry muffin!"

Swithin was in an uncharacteristically merry mood. Everything was going well with the book and he had just decided that he could fit in a week in Italy before term started. A blueberry muffin and a double latte were his way of celebrating.

"Swithin," Keith said, coming toward his table, "we might, just might, need you to help out for a few minutes today. Would that be OK?"

"A few minutes?"

"Well, not long. Today's the day of Beaufort's appearance at the magistrate's court, you know. I'm going to take your advice and go along with him. Ronan is going to stay here. I've known Beaufort for longer. I want to see for myself what's going on—what kind of thing he's supposed to have done."

"I'd go with you," Swithin said, "except that you know him so much better. I hardly know him, but he does seem a perfectly honest, law-abiding citizen."

"He absolutely is!" Fleur exclaimed.

"When is this court appearance to be?" Swithin asked.

"Later this morning," Keith said. "Beaufort is going to come here first, and then we'll go on together. "We're meant to be there for 11:00."

"I like your tie," Fleur said. "You'll make a good impression."

"I hope so. The guy needs whatever support we can give him. I wore this tie when I was Mark's best man."

"I see it survived the reception, Keith," Ronan said, bringing Swithin his coffee and muffin.

"Champagne doesn't really stain, you know. Anyway, the bridesmaid tripped. It couldn't be helped. You make it out to be wilder than it was. Of course it 'survived the reception'!" Swithin had begun to set his books and papers out on his table. "You know," he said, I'll be sorry when the College is ready for use again." His office was being painted pale green, apparently because many hundreds of gallons of pale green paint had been bought.

At exactly 10:15 Beaufort Simmons walked in, also wearing a suit and tie. Instead of being covered by the knitted cap he usually wore, his dreadlocks hung free.

"Hi, Beaufort," Fleur said. "Would you like some of our new mango juice or anything? Before you go?"

"No, girl," he said morosely. "We got to go. Hey, Keith?"

"Right, we can have the juice when we get back," Keith said. "Put your bag in the room there." Beaufort had brought a canvas travel bag with a change of clothes in it.

In a moment they were through the open door and out of Cockaigne Court and off toward the bus stop.

"Well," said Fleur sighing, "I hope it all comes out OK."

Swithin sipped his double latte thoughtfully. "Yes, indeed," he said.

Now and then when people accidentally found The Bohemian Pirate they would remember where it was and manage to find it again. This must have happened for the Dutch "swimming instructor" who had come in once before, because she now came in like an old regular. She got a tuna and sweetcorn sandwich on wholemeal and a latte and sat down at Swithin's table.

"Swidden, isn't it?" she said offering her hand to be shaken. "We have met before."

"Yes, indeed," said Swithin, because the Dutch swimming instructor seemed like one more thing to celebrate on this auspicious day. "Ria?"

"You remembered my name," she said with a warmth in her voice that made Swithin close the book he had been looking at, using his pen as a bookmark. "I must go back to The Nedderlands tomorrow. I've been here with a house swap, and now it is time to go home. I have looked after her cat and she has looked after my cat. I miss my kitchen!"

"What a good way to see another country!" Swithin said.

"Well, I think it is ideal, but you have to be careful. You have to get the right person to come and stay in your house or flat."

"Not just anybody," Swithin said.

"No." Ria took a bite of her sandwich. In a moment she said, "I should tell you about one of my neighbours at home! She does bed and breakfast. She is an elderly widow, and this has been a kind of hobby of hers since many years. She is very careful about the choice of people she has to stay with her. They are usually doctors or professors. She keeps a guest book with all their names and addresses. And then..." she took another bite of her sandwich.

Swithin was imagining this Dutch village with little gabelled houses where Ria and the elderly widow lived.

"And then in the winter season she goes and visits them! By that time they are friends and so they don't charge her anything for a friendly visit.

She has seen a great deal of Germany and Austria in that way. And Holland, too. Some of her bed-and-breakfast guests are from Holland, of course. Amsterdam, Leiden, even Groningen."

Swithin chuckled. "What a very profitable business she has for herself!"

"Yes, but that isn't all," Ria said. "One of her guests was a man called Professor van Amersfoort. He is a retired art historian from Leiden. She went to visit him, too. She began to take a keen interest in art."

"So she was really broadening her horizons, on top of all the travelling," Swithin said, charmed by Ria's accent as much as her story.

"Oh yes, zeker, she talked about Caravaggio as though she knew him personally! She said she never really appreciated Bernini until Professor van Amersfoort explained Italian art to her. For a while she mentioned Tiziano in every conversation. To tell the truth, we got a little tired of it. Titian is very nice when you go to an art gallery, but not endlessly from Mrs. Bakker."

"So this Mrs. Bakker was getting to be a bit of an art expert herself?" Swithin liked Titian, too. He had been to the Uffizi any number of times.

"She was quite artistic anyway. She used to make pottery. She had a kiln in her house. And she weaved, I mean she wove, too. She wove bright covers to throw over her chairs and her sofa. She had an artistic sensibility before she met Professor van Amersfoort. She had a weaving loom in her house, too. You could walk past her house, look in the window, and see her loom with a pretty cloth on it that she was making."

Ria started on the second half of her sandwich and glanced at her watch. "I have to get back to the flat and clean it before I leave tomorrow, but I have some other errands to do first."

Swithin had to get back to his work, too, but he could sit and listen to Ria all day. It was just as well that she didn't have all day.

"Then we didn't see her very much. She used to drop in for a cup of coffee now and then, but there would be weeks and weeks when I didn't see her at all. She was away in Leiden with her Professor. She was calling him Hans now. When you looked into her living room there was the loom with the half-finished cloth on it, and by the window a table with a fruit bowl and an apple that looked worse and worse as the days went on. Finally, Jantje, the neighbour woman who collected her mail and put it on the table where the fruit bowl was, finally she got rid of the apple."

"So did Mrs. Bakker just disappear? Did she ever come back to your village?"

"Town," she corrected him. "Yes, she came back. She seemed very happy. Now there was slightly less about Caravaggio and Tiziano and more about Hans. They were going to get married! Hans was a widower, they had so much in common, she was going to live in Leiden but they were going to get married in our town. We heard all about it."

"But that's nice, if they could make each other happy."

150

"We were happy for her—happy for them. We met him. He was a nice man, maybe a little impressed with himself, or maybe that was just the way he seemed to us. Anyway, they were a nice old couple."

"So! Quite a happy outcome from her bed-and-breakfast hobby! She parlayed her hobby into a whole new life for herself."

"The marriage was announced on the notice board on our town hall. We found out that her full name was Petronella Wilhelmina Emmalina Bakker-Holthorst! That was our Lina, our Linatje! We thought she was seventy-two, too, but that was wrong. She must have subtracted four years from her age at some time in the past, because now we found out that she was really seventy-six!"

"That must have been embarrassing if she had, well, lied about her age and now she was found out!"

"I suppose she realised that she was leaving our town for good and so it didn't matter much whether we knew her real age or not. At some time in the past she lied about her age. I don't know when that was. Perhaps she was forty and said she was thirty-six. Perhaps she was fifty and wanted to stay forty-six. We will never know."

"So she reinvented herself. She defined herself as she wished to be seen by others, and then late in life she took a serious decision about her future."

"Or maybe she didn't take all four years off at the same time. Maybe they came off one by one, or in pairs."

"That was another big change in her life, the late marriage. She decided what she wanted, and then she 'went for it', as they say!"

"Yes," said Ria, "you have to admire her, in a way. She took charge of her own life. I suppose she didn't know where it would lead, did she? She did her b-and-b landlady business, then she made various friends, then she met her Professor van Amersfoort, then they fell in love. You can fall in love at any age, of course. She couldn't have known where it would lead."

"No," said Swithin, you never know where it will lead. You never know where anything will lead."

BEAUFORT'S DAY IN COURT

Keith and Beaufort were back before long, in fact back before they were expected and before Swithin had a chance to fill in behind the counter. The door was still standing open the way Swithin had left it. Keith came in first, closely followed by a smiling Beaufort.

"It looks like you were a good character witness," Fleur said.

"I didn't even have a chance!" Keith said. "Beaufort didn't need me to say what a great guy he is!"

"Well, me glad that over!" said Beaufort. "Now me get on with my life! Got to change me duds." Beaufort went towards the back room.

"They threw the case out!" Keith said. "They threw it out!"

Swithin was almost the only other customer in The Bohemian Pirate. There was a woman at a table some distance away reading The Times. "What happened?" Swithin asked.

"The policeman got it all wrong!" Keith said.

"I knew it!" Fleur said. "There was something wrong somewhere. But what happened in Parliament Square?"

"Well, they were stopping people in a random way. Stopping cars, not pedestrians. Every tenth car or something like that. Maybe every twentieth. They asked people where they were coming from and where they were going."

"So he wasn't, for example, trying to make a right turn out of Whitehall?" Swithin asked.

"Not a bit of it! He was just being Beaufort, going from one of his building jobs in Southwark to another one around Paddington. You know Beaufort." Keith answered. "They stopped him, he had all his work tools in his van—they should have seen that he was a proper workman and not going to do anything dodgy."

"But I distinctly heard Beaufort say he did something wrong in Parliament Square!" Swithin said, trying to see how these loose ends could be made to add up.

"Oh yeah." Keith rolled his eyes. Beaufort did something wrong. How about the policeman?"

"What did he do wrong?" Fleur asked, not quite following the story.

"This cop asked him where he'd been, and Beaufort...Beaufort and his mates had been renovating a Barclay's around Elephant and Castle somewhere, and so Beaufort said...you know Beaufort...he said he was in a hurry and he had just done a bank job!"

There was a pause while they thought how it must have sounded at the time. Fleur hooted with laughter. Swithin allowed himself an extended chuckle.

"So, this cop didn't wait to hear any more!" Keith continued. "Beaufort tried to rephrase it, but everything he said made it look worse, because the cop had it firmly in mind that Beaufort had just confessed to something!"

"As though anyone would confess like that," said Fleur. "Oh, since you ask, I've just robbed a bank."

"Exactly," Keith said. "When Beaufort told us he'd done something wrong, he was embarrassed about being misunderstood. He was too embarrassed to tell us the whole story."

"Poor guy!" Fleur said.

"All he did wrong was to phrase it in this unfortunate way," Swithin remarked.

"Exactly," Keith said again.

"Then what did they say at the magistrate's court?" Fleur asked.

"The presiding magistrate read through the statement and asked Beaufort his name and address and what he did for a living. He saw in a moment what had happened. All three of the magistrates looked at the papers in front of them and burst out laughing. You should have seen the expression on the cop's face. He thought he'd bagged a dangerous criminal!"

Beaufort came out of the back room now and knelt down to do up his shoelaces. "Man, me glad that over!" he said again.

Keith said, "Seriously, they've wasted everybody's time. Look at the way it wrecked Beaufort's whole morning. But Beaufort, I liked the look that magistrate gave the cop! Remember?"

Yeah, that was good," Beaufort said, but it sounded as though he would have happily foregone the whole experience, amusing as it might have been for some.

"This head magistrate stopped laughing," Keith recalled. "He gave the cop such a look! It could have blistered paint. It was a long silent look, and you were in no doubt about the magistrate's opinion of the cop's mental capacity. Something about the way he ever so slightly shook his head. There was a flicker of an eyebrow, like John Gielgud. Did you see that, Beaufort?"

"Yeah, saw it."

"How embarrassing for the chap," Swithin remarked.

"It will teach him to pay more attention to what people say and not jump to conclusions," Fleur said.

"And then," said Keith, "he explained the whole scenario to the rest of the court—these social workers and people waiting for other cases to come up. It brought the house down!"

"It should happen at the Marquis of Granby in Bounds Green!" Fleur said.

"That's definitely where it belonged!" Keith said.

"It was kinda funny, I guess," Beaufort said, standing up. "But that cop was...he was such a banana seed!"

Swithin went back to his table smiling to himself. Maybe it was because Beaufort's outcome was so good that Swithin took up his pen with new zest. Or maybe it was because he was inspired to forge on with that book. Or then again, maybe it was because he was looking forward to that week in Italy. We may never know.

When he finally got back to College—his office now a fresh-smelling willow green—his book was nearly ready to send to the publisher. Elspeth had typed it up on the office computer and knew how to send it to the publisher on a floppy disc. I even asked him once point blank what had made him suddenly get so decisive about applying for a job in California, of all places, and making such a big change in his life. He just shrugged and said he felt that the world was his oyster! You don't expect tired clichés like that from Swithin. I don't know where he picked that up.

6472777R00100

Printed in Great Britain
by Amazon.co.uk, Ltd.,
Marston Gate.